CANDLELIGHT REGENCY SPECIAL

CANDLELIGHT REGENCIES

Oh, What a Tangled Web

Joyce Lee

A Candlelight Regency Special

Published by
Dell Publishing Co., Inc.
1 Dag Hammarskjold Plaza
New York, New York 10017

Dell ® TM 681510, Dell Publishing Co., Inc.

ISBN: 0-440-16821-X

Printed in the United States of America

First printing—August 1981

Oh, what a tangled web we weave,
When first we practise to deceive!

Marmion
Sir Walter Scott

Oh,
What a
Tangled Web

Chapter 1

Until that memorable night of August 10, 1819, it had been more than a hundred years since the ghost of Colter Abbey had walked along the roof of the north wing. But even more remarkable than its reappearance on that date was the dramatic alteration in its person.

His lordship, as the locals referred to the ghost, was the spectral embodiment of Lord Davenant Belcroft, 1st Baron of Belcroft, who had departed this life abruptly one stormy night in 1570 during an energetic dalliance with no less a personage than Good Queen Bess herself.

Her Majesty, in her characteristic manner, accepted the episode with royal aplomb and departed from the abbey on the following morning with nary a backward glance; but Lord Davenant, for several years following the event, raged and blustered nightly across the rooftops, bemoaning in strident howls the loss of his earthly delights.

Little by little, however, as time passed, Lord Davenant's light began to dim. By the year 1592 his voice could no longer be heard, although the stout-hearted, on approaching closely, could still discern movement of the lips and an occasional vehement thrashing of the arms.

By 1620 he had become a resigned specter, merely strolling along the north roof, staring gloomily into space, and on rare occasions tugging at his vaporous beard.

The last sighting was recorded on Christmas eve, 1655, when a young footman and chambermaid from the abbey, both rosy cheeked and flushed with good wine and holiday cheer, had been discovered in the rhododendrons across the garden from the north wing. They stoutly maintained that for almost an hour they had watched his lordship parade solemnly back and forth across the roof, waving a sprig of holly and making signs of the cross. This behavior, while uncharacteristic of Lord Davenant, was accepted as being in keeping with the season, and the appearance was duly noted in the abbey's history.

Thereafter, nothing more was seen of the unhappy baron, although his fame continued to spread throughout the kingdom; and it was not uncommon over the years to encounter young couples in the neighborhood strolling through copses and dells at night, "watching for Lord Davenant."

The weather on the night of August 10, 1819, was perfect for the reappearance of a specter. There was a wind from the sea which brought rain to lash against the windows of the East Study, and an occasional crash of thunder and flare of lightning rent the sky, sending even the hardiest souls scampering to their firesides.

Brandon Belcroft, known to his intimates as Brandy, had chosen the day to entertain two friends on his yacht; and after a heady passage up and down the coast during which they had struggled valiantly against recalcitrant currents, fighting with flapping sails and tightening loose sheets until every muscle rebelled, they had retreated to the East Study of the abbey, where they could warm their chilled members in front of a crackling blaze and administer revivifying potions to their sagging spirits.

Rowan Dillworth, a cherubic young man with a round, shining countenance and a breathless manner, had been especially stimulated by the day's activities.

"Ah, yes," he kept murmuring as he cradled his glass between his hands, inhaling the warm fumes luxuriously, "dashed fine sail, Brandy! Dashed fine sail!" And as he gazed benignly at the streaming windows, he added, "Dashed fine rain, old man. Snug and cozy in here. You couldn't have arranged a better holiday, all 'round."

Then, as he smiled at the downpour against the glass, his eyebrows rose and his smile broadened. "And there's your ghost, by Jove! How jolly of you to add him to the sport. But what's happened to the old boy? You've slipped up, my lad. He's supposed to be a robust gentleman in doublet and hose, and you've turned him into a lithesome young girl. Are you trying to hoax us, old fellow?"

At these words their host, who had been smiling complacently into the fire, leaped out of his chair and rushed to the window. Pressing his face against the pane for a moment, he exclaimed, "Good God!" and rushed out of the room.

The two young men who remained exchanged puzzled glances. Rising, Rowan made his way to the window and peered out; but by this time the apparition, which had been but vaguely discernible before, had disappeared behind a granite urn.

"Hmmm," he mused, "nothing there."

In front of the fire Tristam Gilford, Marquis of Waivering, sat staring morosely into the flames. "If it had been my father's ghost," he sighed, "I should not have been surprised. I'll wager he's a troubled shade at this time."

Rowan went to him quickly and put a hand on his shoulder. "Here now, Tris, you must stop blaming yourself for Lord Ansel's death. How could you possibly have prevented it?"

"If I had been at home, I might have prevailed upon him not to take that fence *all out* on an untried horse."

"Nonsense!" Rowan snorted. "He'd have paid you no heed. Never did listen to you—nor to anyone else, for that matter."

Before Tristam could answer, Brandy came into view outside the window, striding across the roof, his hair pasted down over his face and rain streaming off his nose. A moment later he disappeared behind a curving parapet.

"No one there," Rowan observed. "I say, Tris, do you suppose it's a person who's not meant to be wandering about? The pitiful little sister, perhaps?"

Tristam frowned. "I should not care to speak on

that subject, Ro, unless Brandy mentions the girl himself."

"Yes, yes, quite," Rowan agreed. "Though I can't help wondering why they keep her hidden away, the way they do. Must be something frightfully wrong with her."

Shifting in his chair, Tristam turned to glance uneasily toward the door through which Brandy would return.

"Woodstoke was talking about her just the other day," Rowan went on. "Known the Belcrofts since the year one; said Callie was an exquisite little thing. Would be a charmer now if she were normal. Dash it all, what's the truth about her? I've heard the most astonishing rumors."

"Please, Ro," Tristam protested, "let us speak of something else. Your horses: You're setting up a racing stable, I'm told."

His friend's face brightened. "Yes, indeed. I'm mixing the bloodlines I plotted all those years when I was too down-at-the-heels to buy anything."

"My father would have been interested in your project."

Rowan was frowning again, his thoughts far away. "Would you believe it, Tris, Dum-dum Farlingale said *she* has webbed feet?"

"Good God, man!" Tristam exclaimed, rising up in his chair. "How can you talk like that in this house?"

"Yes, yes," Rowan said quickly. "I shall guard my tongue."

His decision was made none too soon, for a moment later Brandy strode through the doorway, wiping his face with a handkerchief.

"If you'll excuse me a bit, I'll get out of these wet togs," he told them. "And I trust you'll forgive the precipitate manner in which I departed. I feared there would be an accident."

Rowan opened his mouth to speak, hesitated, and turned uncomfortably toward Tristam; then seeing that the marquis was gazing intently into the fire, he steeled himself and continued. "It was not a ghost? Perhaps a living person?"

Brandy hesitated. "Whatever it was, it was gone by the time I arrived on the scene." He frowned and an expression of deep anxiety took possession of his face. "I only wish it had indeed been old Lord Davenant."

The next morning began in its customary way at Colter Abbey: The sun shed a cool radiance over verdant meadows, a fresh zephyr stirred the shrubs as it had done for hundreds of years, and thousands of tiny ornithic throats performed a strident oratorio to greet the day.

Lord Tristam wakened slowly, lying for some time in that half world where reality and dreams merge and carry their subjects on misty barques to distant realms of heavenly bliss or into labyrinths of cruel torment. This day he dozed in a happy state, forgetting for a time that his father was no more.

Today I shall make him proud of me, he thought. *Today I shall mount my new hunter and follow the pack alongside that old curmudgeon, Cavanaugh—*

take the fences along the river in full stride—press over the north Talburn wall with sufficient speed to . . . His thoughts came to an abrupt halt and a tightness constricted his throat. It had been at the north Talburn wall that his father had come to grief.

The tragedy had occurred almost eighteen months before, but Tristam's throat still tightened when the memory caught him unawares. There had been so much left unfinished between him and his father—so many things he had wanted to say before they were separated forever, so many things he had wanted to prove to him. Above all he had wanted to convince Lord Ansel that his son was not a completely inept, bungling ass.

The Marquis of Waivering was, alas, that most unhappy of all creatures, the overgrown, loose-jointed, bumblefooted son of a small, well-coordinated, athletic father. Lord Ansel had been the Corinthian's Corinthian. There had been nothing he could not do as well or better than any other man of his time. When he mounted a horse, he became a centaur; no bird crossed his gunsights with impunity; he was able to mill down men twenty pounds heavier than himself; he held the undisputed record for the Four Horse Club's run to Salt Hill and back.

Tristam, on the other hand, had made his sporting debut by lunging over his pony's back and falling in a heap on the other side, at the feet of no less a personage than Frederick Augustus, Duke of York. He had repeated his performance seven years later when the Elector of Schlesswig-Belzer visited Marcourt with his entourage and Tristam had been especially desirous of earning his father's approval.

By applying himself tirelessly thereafter to the pursuit of perfection, the boy eventually began to gain some skill in the manly arts. While it was discovered that he possessed some aptitude for boxing, these talents never matured, as he was hampered by a strong aversion to inflicting pain on others; but in his early teens he became something of a marksman —after overcoming a predilection for shooting large clumps of foliage out of trees. Unfortunately his father had long since lost any interest he might have had in his son's development and was busily engaged in hunts and shoots and meets which took him as far as possible from his accident-prone offspring.

In his eighteenth year Tristam's muscles and bones finally knitted themselves together. But he and Lord Ansel had suffered so many bitter disappointments over the years that an air of dread pervaded their infrequent meetings, and while both were on tenterhooks waiting for disaster to rear its ugly head and suck the young man into its maw, neither possessed the peace of mind to observe the change that had taken place in him, or the change in the attitude of the world around him. They remained unaware that he now presented a rather splendid picture on his enormous hunter, his six-foot-five-inch frame stylishly encased in impeccable togs by Stultz and every well-schooled muscle at last performing efficiently. His face, which had always been rather dark and equine, had grown up to its teeth; and so pleasing had his appearance become that his entrance at Carlton House during the Regent's fete on July 21, 1814, in honor of the Duke of Wellington, had brought forth an exclamation from Lord Osgood Belcroft.

"Good God, Ans!" he observed to his friend. "That boy of yours has grown to be devilish handsome! I never expected him to be so comely, I assure you."

Lord Ansel turned languidly to survey his son, holding a quizzing glass to his right eye. "Well, by God, you're right, Os. Now, if only he may find a way to comport himself with some degree of style—perhaps become a dashing blade among the ladies—and wipe away some of the memories of his childish disasters . . ."

Alas, it was not meant to be. Like the dutiful son he was, Tristam had, from an early age, taken over the management of the Waivering estates for his peripatetic sire, and he was rarely in town, where he might have acquired polish and shed his diffident manner. And so thorough had been the depression of his pretensions during childhood that he continued to walk quietly through life, oblivious to the world's changing attitude toward him. Once when Rowan told him pointblank that he was a "dashed fine-looking chap," he had silenced him with an impatient, "Rubbish!"

"I have never been concerned with such nonsense as appearance," he added. "It is *performance* which counts. And God knows I've been a cursed failure in that quarter. Someday, however, in some manner, I shall contrive to convince my father that I am a human being worthy of his regard."

17

Lord Ansel's untimely demise on the far side of the north Talburn wall had put an end to those hopes, and for a time Tristam had appeared to be so shattered by his father's death that his mother, Lady Gracia, had feared for his reason. He spent long weeks wandering silently over his estates, often declining to speak for days at a time. Finally, when his mother had begun to despair of his ever recovering, he slowly returned to his normal behavior—although that was sufficiently melancholy to alarm most parents.

"Thank heaven," Lady Gracia remarked to a friend, "I have not lost both husband and son. The boy is at last putting his father out of his mind."

But Tristam's father was often in his thoughts. He particularly brooded over the injustice of his father's death while other, less worthy souls were allowed to live. On that fateful morning of August 11, as he lay watching the sunlight fall in sparkling rays, fragmented into showers of stars by the carved panes of glass in the leaded casements, and the gentlest of breezes wafted a fragrance of citrus blossoms from the greenhouses while the rolling, glittering contata of a thousand avian voices filled the air, he could not but be aware that a glorious day was approaching. He scowled.

"Blast this wretched earth!" he muttered as he threw back the covers. "How can it have the audacity to flaunt such beauty when my father is not here to enjoy it?"

Chapter 2

Lord Tristam elected to dispense with the services of his valet and dress himself, as he desired a few more minutes in his own silent company. Then letting himself quietly out of the house, he set off on a vigorous tramp down a woodsy path to the lake. When he reached its graveled shore, he proceeded briskly around its perimeter, then back to the house, deep in thought.

Several weeks before, he had been obliged to accept some basic truths about himself and his situation. He had realized that, no matter what triumphs he might achieve in the future, there was nothing which could nurture his self-esteem as satisfactorily as a simple word of praise from his father would have done. However, it also occurred to him that there were still methods by which he could achieve peace of mind. What he must do, he realized, was to perform a feat which would inspire society to exclaim, "What a fortunate chap Lord Ansel was to have had such a son!" This public acclaim, he felt certain, would have elicited words of approval from his father's lips, and thus would, in a roundabout way, satisfy himself.

No sooner had he arrived at this conclusion than he set about trying to hit upon a project which would rocket him spectacularly into the hearts of the English public. After cudgeling his brains for some time, he came to the conclusion that the ways in which he could most easily impress the world were twofold: He could quadruple his fortune overnight, or he could invent a marvelous device which would change the course of history.

Having arrived at this conclusion, he reasoned that the simpler of the two approaches would be to devise a method for multiplying his fortune; but after considering and discarding several promising notions—each of which threatened to plunge him into penury if the tiniest miscalculation were committed —he concluded that such a road to celebrity was much too risky for a person of his temperament. He then put his mind to the task of inventing a wonderful new device.

He rapidly discarded as impracticable a sprinkler which could be attached to carriages for the reduction of dust throughout the city, and a lighting system which would provide, by the simple flick of a switch, ample and clean illumination.

But he continued to muse on one of the most pressing problems from which England still suffered —the atrocious condition of its roads—and it occurred to him that if John Loudon Macadam's methods were extended and highways were reconstructed with an even tighter, more durable material than gravel, it would be possible for the thoroughfares to preserve a hard, smooth surface for a much longer period of time, and as the result of developing such a process the inventor's name would soon be on everyone's lips. By the time he paid his visit to Colter Abbey, Tristam was busy attempting to formulate a method by which crushed seashell could be applied. The main problem was to select a binding agent which would be durable, waterproof, inexpensive, and available in large quantities. He was considering linseed oil, and as he strode along the path from Abbey Lake, he attempted to calculate the length of time it would require to dry. If an oil painting required one week to harden a layer which was as thick as a sheet of paper, how long would be necessary to dry a layer which was as thick as five hundred sheets? Five hundred weeks! No, no, that could not be correct! Besides, the same conditions would not obtain in this situation.

He had stopped at one of the abbey's rear entrances and was scowling to himself, trying to think of a quick-drying binder which might be substituted for linseed oil, when he became aware of a sound. Raising his face, he looked around and realized, for the first time, that he was standing on a singularly beautiful terrace which was obviously very old. It terminated in a low, ornate balustrade at either end, beyond which were clusters of bushes blooming in glorious chaos. The walls of the abbey were of the local stone, roughly cut and laid together, and they were pierced by windows of random sizes and glazing methods which had been inserted at various periods of history on the whims of its inhabitants.

Observing no signs of life nearby which might have produced the sound, Tristam examined the wall of the house, appreciatively taking in the harmony which had somehow been achieved despite its disparate parts. Eventually his gaze traveled up to a small oval window which had been inserted high under the eaves. It was encircled by a beaded frame, and in its center, reflecting light as though it were a small jeweled brooch, was the most exquisite face he had ever seen.

For a moment he stared at it, wondering if it were painted on the glass. Then he wondered if it were, perhaps, carved, as it resembled a cameo with fine porcelain skin cut smoothly out of a darker mother stone.

For several seconds the face remained immobile, staring fixedly into space. Then, to his surprise, it moved, turning to look down at him solemnly. He took a step backward, tilting his head to obtain a better view. Slowly the image's lips parted in an elfin smile.

Tristam stared. He was about to return the smile when, to his consternation, the face dimmed abruptly and disappeared. For several minutes he waited for it to reappear, his head tilted back and his neck rapidly developing a crick. When it became apparent that the apparition had permanently withdrawn, he began to muse on its owner. The mysterious sister, perhaps, he conjectured. Rubbing his brow thoughtfully, he tried to remember what Dum-dum Farlingale had said about her—something that pertained to ducks, as he recalled.

He shook his head and tried to put thoughts of her out of his mind as he reentered the house and made his way back to his bedroom. But the memory of the face kept popping into his consciousness as his valet readied him for the morning's activities, and by the time he left his bedroom and made his way thoughtfully down the stairs, he was determined to speak to Brandy and discover, as discreetly as possible, what sort of mystery it was that surrounded the girl.

Rowan Dillworth was jarred out of sleep at an early hour by a cacophony of twittering cries from the trees outside his windows. He endeavored for some time to sink back into the arms of Morpheus, but failing, at last sat up in bed, muttering to himself, and summoned his valet. When he marched out of his room some half hour later, he made his way, he thought, in the direction of the main staircase. But some time later, after walking briskly into a linen closet, then finding himself in a corridor which was festooned with cobwebs and over which hung an eerie silence, he was relieved to turn into another hallway and find Tristam also wandering about in search of his breakfast.

Joining forces, they made their way together along a shallow tunnel which proved to lead onto a scullery. There they were peering into the room, hoping to find a servant who might send them in the right direction, when they were discovered by a large gray cat which came away from a milk crock, licking a creamy white substance from its chops. It beamed up at them, rumbled hospitably, and after leaning affectionately against Tristam's boots, then Rowan's, accompanied them on their search, winding itself in and out among their feet, much to the peril of them all. After a number of additional false turns the little party at last arrived in the doorway of a small solarium on the south side of the house, where they found their handsome host and hostess at table. Lord Osgood and Lady Regina, each seated at one end of a long table, were scowling fiercely at each other. Her ladyship was trembling.

"If you think for one moment that I shall submit to such vile treatment, you wicked . . . you *evil* man . . ." she cried in a strangled voice. And she slammed down her coffee cup with such violence that its contents sloshed onto the table.

Tristam, momentarily taken aback by the scene into which he had blundered, recoiled a step and trod on the cat's tail. With a piercing scream that offended creature fled down a hallway into the darkness while Lady Regina, starting violently, swung around to face the new arrivals. For a moment she gaped at them, her eyes goggling; then her face wreathed itself in smiles.

"Ah, Lord Tristam!" she caroled in the sweetest of voices. "And dear Rowan. Come take these chairs on either side of me. How delightful to have two sprightly young gentlemen to enliven our conversation." She turned to her husband and gave him a speaking look. "Colter Abbey has been abysmally dull these past few weeks."

Lord Osgood bared his teeth in a broad grin. "It has indeed! Tedious, dull, and boring!"

Her ladyship's nose quivered. "Sir," she began in a voice which was redolent with stifled emotion, "if you mean to continue . . ."

Suddenly she stopped, glanced toward Tristam and Rowan, mused for a moment, then straightened her face and contrived a fresh smile. "Yes, yes, of course, my dear, whatever you say." She patted the chairs on either side of her.

The two young gentlemen, casting nervous glances from their host to their hostess, gingerly seated themselves. As they were settling into their chairs, the Belcrofts' butler entered with a silver tray and offered it to his master.

"Regina," Lord Osgood muttered, scowling down at the plate, "these kidneys are overdone again. How can Cook expect me to eat them when they're as dry as rocks?"

Lady Regina raised her eyebrows innocently. "Dear, dear," she exclaimed, "has Cook spoiled them again? After twenty-eight years one would expect her to get them right." She waved a hand at the butler. "Please, Rimpson, be very firm with Cook. Tell her that this sort of thing will not do at all. Tell her that his lordship is not satisfied. He says the kidneys are overdone."

"*Not satisfied!*" Osgood cried. "*He says* . . . I tell you the kidneys are dry and overcooked! Anyone but a halfwit can see at a glance that they are not as they should be."

"Of course, my love," she chirped. "They are the

driest, most unpalatable kidneys we have ever served. I do not doubt your word."

Lord Osgood sat grimly munching his jaws as Rimpson fled with the plate of kidneys. Smiling graciously, Lady Regina turned to Lord Tristam.

"Now, sir," she said, "shall we put aside all unpleasant thoughts on this glorious day? I shall prevail upon you to give me the latest news of your mother —one of my dearest friends when I was a girl. My bitterest regret is that my duties and hers constantly exile us from each other's company."

"These eggs are too dry," Osgood muttered, pushing away a dish which a footman was proffering.

"Good heavens, Rimpson!" Lady Belcroft snapped at the unfortunate butler, who had been so improvident as to reenter the room and was standing poised in the doorway, a stricken expression on his face. "Take all this rubbish away and bring his lordship something he'll eat. How long can we endure this incessant carping?"

Osgood placed both hands on the table and raised himself halfway out of his chair.

"*Incessant carping*, madam? How dare you imply that I am never satisfied!"

"But my dearest one," she assured him with a brittle tinkle of laughter, "I have implied no such thing. I have known you to be satisfied several times during the past twenty years."

With a stiff smile and nod of her head to Tristam then Rowan she picked up a roll and with great deliberation fell to buttering it, spreading the lubricant briskly back and forth, smoothing it into a uniform layer, then, dissatisfied, gathering it into a tiny windrow and spreading it out again. Osgood, watching her sullenly, sank back into his chair.

"Must you do that?" he growled.

"Do what?" she asked, looking up in surprise.

"Moosh your butter back and forth. It's a detestable habit you have. Certainly you were taught in the schoolroom that it is an abominable practice to moosh, moosh, moosh your butter. It must be slid on quickly, with the least possible flourish, then the roll popped into the mouth in small pieces, drawing as little attention as possible to the mechanics of eating. It's enough to make a person violently ill to watch you strop, strop, strop with your butter knife, ad infinitum."

Lady Regina, who had struggled to her feet and was shaking with fury, cried, "Moosh! Stop!"

At that moment Brandy entered the room, his face a mask of contentment after a good night's sleep. He nodded happily to Rowan, then to Tristam; but as his glance fell on his mother's trembling form and his father's scowling face, he stopped in alarm and stared from one parent to the other.

"Mama!" he protested.

"Yes, yes, my dear," Osgood agreed, yawning elaborately toward his wife and patting a graceful hand over his mouth. "Sit down, I beg of you. Our guests have no desire to witness one of your picturesque little scenes."

Lady Regina, gritting her teeth, was changing color rapidly as she employed her last ounce of strength to control herself. But suddenly her resolve collapsed. With a quick, deft motion, she caught up her roll and flung it at the head of her spouse. That gentleman, eyes widening, was momentarily tempted to maintain his dignity at all costs, and sat stiffly in his place, scornfully watching the roll's approach. At the last moment, however, his courage failed him and he ducked. The roll, providentially arriving buttered-side-to, grazed the top of his forehead and stuck fast among his artistically tumbled locks. Regina's face brightened. She let out a wild trill of laughter.

"Oh, sir!" she cried. "What a pretty picture you present!"

Lord Osgood's expression clouded. He cautiously raised a hand to explore his head, muttering darkly as his fingers encountered the roll. Grasping the offending missile, he lowered it to his plate.

"Ugh," he murmured, wiping his hand on a napkin, "how anyone can stomach such excess!" He bared his teeth again in a fixed smile and wagged a finger playfully at his wife. "My dear, you'll soon be as fat as a pumpkin if you continue to imbibe such quantities of grease. I have been meaning to warn you that I have detected the veriest hint of a tiny extra chin beginning to form beneath your original exquisite one."

"Sir . . ." Brandy pleaded.

Osgood blotted his mouth elaborately with his napkin and, rising, bowed ceremoniously to Brandy and his two white-faced friends.

"Yes, yes, I am aware that there is a certain air of friction in this room; so I shall withdraw and seek the peace and tranquility of the fabled bards of yore. Please send Rimpson to the library with my breakfast when it is properly prepared." And with a nod to the gentlemen, pointedly ignoring his wife, he strolled indolently from the room.

Lady Regina stood scowling after him, her lips twitching; but suddenly she made a sound in her throat which resembled a suppressed giggle and, sinking back into her chair, turned toward her son, grinning mischievously at him.

"Mama!" he chided. "You are the very worst sort of scamp."

"I know," she agreed. "But such a sight he made with my roll protruding from the front of his hair, like a great, blazing lantern. It was too delightful." And she went off into peals of laughter.

Brandy clicked his tongue disapprovingly and, seating himself, gestured for the footman to serve his guests. Lady Regina sighed.

"To think that Osgood was the catch of the Season, the year I came out. So much in love we were too. I should have been much wiser to have married Lord Ansel instead."

She nodded toward Tristam; but as he turned a startled face toward her, she added hastily, "Of course, that would not have been possible, as your father was so besotted with dear Gracia that he was not aware of any other young girl's existence."

Tristam smiled.

Lady Regina's face brightened suddenly, and she turned to Rowan. "I see now that I should have penetrated your uncle's defenses, my dear, and

29

charmed him into marriage. Such a pleasure it would have been to spend his vast wealth."

Rowan chuckled. "Yes, I must confess I'm enjoying it myself."

"Indeed, you must be," Lady Regina agreed. "How happy we were to hear of your good fortune. What, pray tell, are you doing with your inheritance?"

"I have purchased Meadowmere," he told her. "It's a marvelous old house with great potential. I have already added a reflecting pool which will give it a look of Versailles."

"How delightful!" Lady Regina exclaimed, clasping her hands.

"I also had thought to contrive a ruined cathedral peeping out of the beechwood park," he continued. "I spoke to my architect about it; but he is in favor of a ruined chapel instead. What is your opinion?"

"A chapel would be the thing, of course," Regina said with finality. "So much more charm than a cathedral."

Rowan sighed. "I should have liked a cathedral, but I shall bow to your superior taste. It is my wish that when I have finished refurbishing Meadowmere, it will not provoke disgust even from the Prince Regent himself."

"How delightful it is all going to be, to be sure," Lady Regina agreed. "I should like to see it when it is finished."

"Should you?" he exclaimed. Then he sobered. "It may never be finished, ma'am. I plan to continue making improvements throughout my entire lifetime. But I should be highly honored if you were to pay a visit and give your most expert advice on our future construction. I have wondered whether I should add a formal garden on the lower terrace."

Lord Tristam, whose thoughts had wandered back to the face in the cameo window, roused at the word *terrace*. "Yes, yes," he said quickly. "There is a very fine terrace here at Colter Abbey. You should perhaps take it for your model, Ro. And I saw the most beautiful girl looking out of a little round window there." He turned to his host. "Was it your sister perhaps, Brandy?"

His host smiled. "Indeed, it may have been. Would you care to meet her?"

"No, no!" Regina exclaimed. "Impossible! The poor child is ill."

"Is she, indeed?" Brandy asked in surprise. "She was perfectly well last evening."

"Yes," Regina insisted, "but this morning she was suffering from . . . well, who knows what? The doctor is on his way. I fear it may be mumps."

"Mumps! But she had mumps when she was six years old," Brandy reminded his mother. "It's not possible to contract them more than once."

"Measles, then," Regina suggested.

Brandy frowned at her. He would have spoken, but she silenced him with a tiny movement of the left hand. She cleared her throat.

"Yes, I collect it is the measles, or something of the sort. You know how these children are, with first one complaint and then another." She turned to smile at her two young guests. "But certainly you must meet her one day when she is out of the school-room. You will enjoy her pretty little ways—and of course she will find both of you delightful."

"Of course," Brandy agreed. "I do not wish to sound boastful, but my sister is a delightful girl. Pretty . . . sweet-tempered . . ."

"She lives very quietly, however," Lady Regina interrupted. "Her health is frail."

Brandy shook her head. "Not so frail that she cannot enjoy some of the entertainments the *ton* has to offer. Perhaps next Season . . ."

"Perhaps," Lady Regina said quickly.

"Yes, yes," Rowan said, his face pink with embarrassment. "By that time I collect she shall be rid of her measles."

Chapter 3

"Sir Tristam was a dark and brooding knight . . ." Callie began, reading aloud from the well-worn tome which lay open on her lap. She hesitated and slowly raised her face to gaze out through the cameo window and across the lily pond at the flickering ripples of sunlight that shimmered on its surface. "A dark and brooding . . ." she repeated softly to herself.

And he was precisely that, the Marquis of Waivering. She had first caught sight of him the night before, while he was striding along the main corridor toward the East Study. Fortunately he had turned his face away to glance at the rain which was streaming down the windowpanes, and she had been able to step quickly back into the shadows of the intersecting hallway and thence behind a drapery, where she could watch him unobserved.

At first she had been struck by his remarkable height, and the thick black chunks of hair which he kept raking back from his brow with impatient fingers. She had then observed the expression on his dark, pensive face, and her heart had shivered with sympathy. Never had she seen such sadness in a young man's eyes.

"He is the most romantic figure!" she had informed her abigail as the girl prepared her for bed. "Some crushing tragedy has left him with this wonderful look of patient suffering."

"Poor young gentleman," the abigail agreed. "It's his father's death that makes him so grim."

Callie bristled. "How can that be true, Polly? The loss of a parent is a serious blow, but it does not evoke the sort of expression which clouds Lord Tristam's brow. I collect he is suffering from a stunning disappointment in love."

"No, he ain't," the girl insisted. "Your own high-in-the-instep Miss Rempe says he lives very quiet—always has. Never mingles much with the ton and never yet attached his fancy to a young lady. It was his father's death what nearly upset his reason—and he's still brooding over it. Everyone says so."

Callie frowned.

Polly brushed her mistress's hair gently back from her forehead. "It's better this way, love, don't you see? His heart's still in one piece and ripe for the plucking. Why don't you set your cap for him? He's a grand-looking gentleman, and a marquis—rich as Croesus, they say—a quiet, sort of soft-spoken chap who'd overlook your affliction, like as not."

Callie shook her head firmly. "I do not intend to *pluck* anyone's heart—and I cannot like the phrase, Polly. Besides . . ." She was silent for a moment, then lied, "Lord Tristam has not precisely caught my fancy."

However, after the girl had left her, she had found herself thinking of him uninterruptedly, and she had fallen asleep wondering what sort of person he was . . . what sort of activities amused him . . . what sort of company he preferred . . .

The following morning she had found herself again preoccupied with thoughts of him. Before the rest of the house was awake, she had risen and dressed herself, then crept up to her secret room high under the eaves. She had been curled up, endeavoring to concentrate on one of the enormous old tomes which had been in the library since the abbey was a holy place, when she had glanced out of the cameo window and discovered the man himself below her on the terrace, striding purposefully up and down, a thoroughly romantic scowl on his face.

While she watched him, he had marched to the end of the brickwork and paused to stare into space. Swinging off his hat with one hand, he had run his fingers through his hair, in the same abstracted manner he had effected the night before. Then, snapping the hat against his thigh, he had turned and strode the other way, drawing himself up at the opposite balustrade and standing for a moment to contemplate the vista which spread itself in misty tiers of woodland beyond the nearby shrubbery. With the sunlight falling full on his crown his rumpled locks were rich with heavy blue shadows. He had turned slowly and started back across the terrace.

Halfway to the other railing he had paused and abruptly raised his eyes to examine the face of the building. Caught unaware, Callie would have ducked out of sight, but her curiosity triumphed over timidity. He was staring up at her so steadily that she felt a little ripple of excitement. Without considering what she did, she smiled.

Her mood was broken immediately by her governess. "Miss Callie!" the woman exclaimed, striding into the room through a door in the opposite wall. "What are you doing? Is one of your brother's friends below on the terrace?"

Flushing with embarrassment, Callie drew away from the window, wondering if Miss Rempe's stentorian voice had carried to Lord Tristam's ears.

"Indeed," the woman continued, her faded brows drawn into a supercilious scowl, "after your escapade last night—and it is a wonder you did not fall to your death or at the very least contract an inflamation of the lungs from wandering about in the rain—I should think you would be happy to avoid any form of excitement which might send you roaming over the rooftops again tonight."

"I do not intend to wander anywhere tonight, ma'am," Callie retorted through tight lips.

"Indeed, miss!" Rempe challenged her. "Indeed?"

"Yes, indeed, ma'am," she replied, her face instantly flushing red with embarrassment at her own rudeness.

"Well!" Miss Rempe snapped. "Your reply does not do you credit, miss. I shall speak to your parents."

Callie tightened her lips still more and stared back at her defiantly.

"It is my duty at this time to warn you most

urgently against imbuing any of your brother's friends with storybook attributes. A young lady in your unenviable position must put all romantic nonsense out of her head. Your parents shall make all arrangements for you: They'll find a suitable gentleman for you to marry when the time is right—a mature person, certainly, of compassion and understanding, who will already have produced an heir. Your fine dowry . . ."

"I will not listen to speculation on my future, Miss Rempe," Callie cut in. "I am extremely tired and wish to be alone here. I shall appreciate it very much if you will be so kind as to leave me."

The governess drew herself up haughtily. "I shall speak to your mother about this, miss."

"Please do," Callie said.

For a moment they stood glaring into each other's flushed, indignant faces. Then with a snort Miss Rempe marched out of the room. Callie quickly closed the door behind her and locked it. Resettling herself in the window seat, she peered down onto the terrace. Tristam was no longer in sight. With a heavy sigh she pulled the tome back onto her lap, relocated the page she had been reading, and focused her eyes on the words. But they quickly blurred, and her thoughts wandered back to the Marquis of Waivering's brooding face.

I wonder . . . she thought.

She was roused some time later by a knock on the door and the sound of her brother's voice.

"Callie!" he called. "Open this door immediately! Are you all right?"

"Yes, of course," she called back, stretching her stiffened limbs and pushing the tome off her lap. The leg she had been sitting on tingled wildly as she hobbled across the room.

"What's wrong?" Brandy asked, stepping quickly inside. "Why did you lock yourself into this room?"

She pulled the door closed behind him and again turned the key. "Because Rempe is plaguing me to death! Brandy, is there no way to be rid of the woman? She is certainly the most tactless person in the entire world! Today she had the audacity to tell me that my affliction is hopeless and my parents will be obliged to find a kindly old man to marry me, one who will only care for my dowry and who will already have an heir, not wishing to mingle our blood with his."

"Good God!" Brandy exclaimed. "What monumental gall!"

"But what makes it especially painful is that I know she is right," Callie told him, her eyes filling with tears. "This wretched affliction of mine is the most dreadful burden for all of you!"

Brandy scowled. "Why must you insist on referring to it as an *affliction?* Sleepwalking is not an affliction; it is a mere inconvenience, nothing more. Most children suffer from such annoyances and quickly outgrow them."

"I am no longer a child, Brandy. I fear this aberration is the harbinger of madness, the result of our relationship to old King Charles the Mad of France —and our parents fear it too."

"Nonsense!"

"No, it is true," she insisted. "I have resigned myself to the fact that there is no future for me in the real world. I am going to enter a nunnery."

"What!" he cried, starting violently. "What are you saying? A nunnery, indeed! You are not even of a religious turn of mind."

"But if I spent long hours in prayer," she argued, "perhaps I should acquire a vocation. Besides, I should be confined at night and unable to wander about, frightening people."

Brandy began to pace angrily back and forth in front of her. "That it should come to this! Our parents must accept the blame and rectify this terrible situation. You know perfectly well, Callie, that it is their bitter quarrels which upset you so profoundly and send you wandering at night in search of peace."

"No," she said softly, "I think not, Brandy. I fear it is the sign of an unbalanced mind."

He threw up both hands. "This is the most outrageous nonsense! How did you hit upon the idea of retiring to a nunnery, pray?"

"Miss Rempe . . ." she began.

"That odious woman! There is no end to her mischief! But with that gabbling tongue of hers I hesitate to turn her out—there is no telling what fantastic tales she may manufacture and spread about the countryside."

"If she tells the truth, we shall be undone," Callie noted, sinking unhappily back onto the window seat.

Brandy settled himself on an ancient chair beside her and took her hand firmly in his.

"I wish you to put this nonsense out of your head

once and for all. You are a perfectly normal, level-headed girl; and I blame myself for allowing matters to come to such a pass. Now I shall take a stand with my parents and in six months—six months only—I promise you that I shall turn your life about. I shall see that it is filled with warmth and hope, to replace the misery you are now enduring."

"But how can you do that?"

"I shall take you to London at once, and there you shall join in all sorts of delightful activities. You shall visit places of interest—like the Tower and the British Museum. You shall ride in the park, attend delightful parties—in short, enjoy the company of other cheerful, optimistic, delightful young people. And as soon as you are busy and happy, I promise you, this sleepwalking business will end."

Callie hesitated, looking up at him hopefully. Then her brow tightened. "But if you believe me to be sane, Brandy, why did you not present me to your friend who has been visiting here?"

"Rowan? If only I had done so. He's a wonderfully cheerful fellow—the perfect sort of man for you, I swear. I shall encourage a match between the two of you."

"It was not Rowan I was thinking of," she told him. "It was your other friend. I saw him walking on the terrace, and he had such a courteous air."

"Tristam? Yes, of course, he is an excellent chap. And he asked about you. I was on the point of calling you in and introducing you all around, but Mama said you were ill today—suffering from mumps or measles."

"Mumps or measles!" Callie cried, leaping to her feet indignantly. "How could you believe such a thing? I am no longer subject to such childish complaints."

"After your little walk across the roofs last night I thought you might have been indisposed. A touch of fever, perhaps."

"I am never a victim of fever."

"So you see? You are a remarkably healthy young lady. And if we provide you with entertainment and fresh interests, you shall be happy and peaceful, and sleep in your bed at night as you are meant to do. I am going to speak to Mama and Papa immediately about removing to town."

"But the Season is past," Callie reminded him.

"No matter. Aunt Seffronia will know what to do to entertain you, living in town all the year round, as she does. And we shall leave Rempe here at the abbey, safely tucked away where her tongue can do no harm."

He patted her hand affectionately. "Be of good cheer, Callie; a whole new world of happiness is opening up for you."

She frowned. "What if you cannot convince our parents?"

"I shall convince them, never fear!" he told her.

"Are you mad!" Lady Regina exclaimed. "Take Callie to town? Never! She will begin to wander about immediately and may even march out into the square, in full view of the world. Or she may fall to her death from a window or the roof—the house

41

there has not been altered to keep her inside at night."

"We can easily remedy that," Brandy pointed out.

"But no!" she insisted. "The London servants will gossip, and then the terrible truth will be out."

"But that is just the point, Mama," he told her. "The truth is not so terrible as you seem to believe."

"It is dreadful!" she cried, pressing a hand over her heart. "It is the most humiliating thing that has happened to this family in years."

Brandy shook his head. "Only humiliating for you, because you know that your constant quarreling with my father is the root of her trouble."

"What!" she cried. "What insolence is this? If you think I shall allow my son to . . ."

"Mama," Brandy interrupted in a voice which was low-pitched but sufficiently penetrating to rivet his mother's attention, "I have spoken to my father, and he has agreed to let me have my way. Now I shall say the same things to you that I have said to him. If you wish to go to town as a family and reopen Belcroft House, then we shall all go together and make an effort to bring Callie out of her mopes. If you do not wish to go, I shall take her to Aunt Seffronia. In either event I shall devote myself wholeheartedly to my sister's safety, and I guarantee that she will not be allowed to walk out a window or off the edge of a roof. And I am confident that as soon as she has some pleasant diversion and is put in a happy frame of mind, her sleepwalking will cease."

Regina shook her head. "Never!" she said. "Under

no circumstances will I ever be prevailed upon to take that gentle, stricken child into the world!"

Chapter 4

The letter announcing the arrival in town of the Belcroft family was waiting for Rowan when he returned from Lady Claemoor's musicale. It had been an evening of mixed blessings, and he had fared rather badly as the result of a lengthy performance by a "delightful new light on the musical horizon." As a cushion against some rather penetrating high notes which had wrought havoc on his nervous system, Rowan had imbibed rather more freely of the punch than he had intended; and when he walked up his own front steps, he deplored the fact that he had arrived home so quickly—another few blocks of vigorous striding, he felt, would have cleared his head properly.

It was, therefore, with mounting pleasure that his eye ran down the page of Brandy's epistle, and he called to Foster to bring him his hat and gloves again.

"Bless me if Mr. Brandon has not come to town," he told his butler. "I shall trot over to Belcroft House and have a few words with him."

Back in the street he made his way briskly around

the square, breathing deeply and exhaling with considerable force in an effort to stir his circulation and flush his system of a certain fogginess which still held possession of his head. He was puffing and blowing industriously as he rounded the corner. But as Belcroft House came into view directly in front of him, he drew up with a jerk, and his breath stuck in his throat. There, flickering across the roof, was the ghost of Colter Abbey.

There could be no doubt about it—it was the same ghost, exactly as he had beheld her on the night of the storm. Slender and graceful, with a face and flowing hair that were as white as mist in the moonlight, she was floating steadily along the edge of the eaves toward the corner of the building. Rowan watched her, mouth agape, waiting for her to reach the end of the roof, where she would drift off into space and dissolve in the cool night air.

But suddenly another figure burst into view, scrambling through a garret window, and Brandy's voice could be heard calling in anguished tones, "Callie! Come back! Please, love, come see what I'm holding in my hand. Callie! I have a kitten here. Come see how soft it is. Callie!"

She continued, unhesitating, on her way.

"Please!" he begged. "Good God, Callie, please come back!"

He began to crawl along in the phantom's wake, balancing himself precariously on the sloping roof. "Please, Callie," he moaned. "You don't want me to fall, do you? Come see what I have in my hands."

Watching him, Rowan had turned cold. In three

more steps the girl would be off the end of the roof, plunging to certain death on the stone pavement below, and it was only with the utmost difficulty that Brandy was maintaining his foothold on the slippery tiles. In a moment, Rowan thought, he too would slide off the other side.

"Please, Callie," he begged. "Please! For Brandy's sake."

She hesitated.

"Come along and see all the pretty things I've bought for you," he urged. "Some silks and laces for a new dress—and a shiny black pony to ride in the park. Come look."

Suddenly—just as Rowan had given up hope—the girl turned and drifted back along the edge of the rain gutter. Brandy reached out his hand and guided her up the slates, then in through the window. No sooner was she safe inside than he scrambled after her. But the moment he had planted his feet firmly on the floor, he sank onto the windowsill and leaned against the jamb, his forearm braced against it and his face buried inside his elbow. His shoulders began to shake violently.

Rowan took a deep, shuddering breath; to his surprise he discovered that he had not inhaled for some time and his ears were ringing. Brandy was still leaning against the jamb, his shoulders bowed and his face turned away. Softly Rowan backed out of sight behind some bushes. His head, he discovered, was now thoroughly cleared and his blood rushed vigorously through his veins.

* · * *

46

After his experience on the terrace of Colter Abbey Lord Tristam found himself, much to his discomfort, the victim of an obsession. He could not rid himself of the vision he had beheld in the window of that noble old house. At regular intervals throughout the day the misty image would pop into his head, obliging him to pause in his activities while his thoughts drifted away on flights of happy fantasy. When he found himself beginning to incorporate the girl into his dreams of the future, however, he gave himself a vigorous shake and stopped to take stock of the situation.

He dimly remembered having heard, in the past, other gossip besides Rowan's which dealt with the Belcroft girl. One summer his cousin Elizabeth had been visiting Marcourt and had entertained a young friend, Melinda Gilbrandice. The two girls had spent much of their time whispering and giggling together, and Tristam had heard the mumbled name Callie Belcroft several times while the maidens rolled their eyes and clasped their hands in horror. Disgusting behavior, he had thought at the time, and he had expressed his disapproval in his customary way, informing them curtly that their actions were disgraceful, then drawing himself up to his full height and scowling at them. For some reason—he had been startled at the time—Miss Gilbrandice had become quite alarmed; the conversation had come to an abrupt halt, and she had fled into the garden. Elizabeth, rushing after her, had called indignantly over her shoulder, "Honestly, Tristam! You odious creature!"

Later, at a dancing party, the Witherspoon chit had given him a sly smile and said, "Lord Tristam, have you heard the latest on-dit about Callie Belcroft?" He had scowled down at her in his most forbidding manner and said, "There is nothing I despise more than gossip, Miss Witherspoon. I shall be highly displeased if you repeat it to me."

Now he wished he had listened, for no matter how he cudgeled his brains, he could not imagine a single word which could be uttered in disparagement of so lovely a girl. After musing on the problem for an entire afternoon he decided to discuss the matter with his mother.

Striding into the north sitting room shortly before tea time, he found Lady Gracia seated in front of a bow window, gazing out into the rose garden, an expression of resigned melancholy on her still pretty face.

"Ah, my dearest," she called to him, a smile warming her eyes, "come sit with me a moment before tea is brought in."

He planted a perfunctory kiss on her cheek and sank himself absentmindedly onto a chair which was much too small for him.

"What do you know of Callie Belcroft?" he began without preamble. "Regina's daughter."

Gracia opened her mouth, then closed it and munched thoughtfully on her back teeth.

"Very little, actually. I've heard the rumor, of course, and lately received hints of other dark doings at Colter Abbey, though most of the gossips hesitate to share their tidbits with me, knowing I've been

48

Seffronia's bosom bow all my life—Regina's good friend also for many years."

"What is the rumor you've heard?" he asked her.

"Only the birthmark."

"Birthmark?" he said, straightening himself in his chair.

"Yes. She inherited it from the French Valois king Charles VI. It proves that she is the one and only, undisputed heir to the throne."

Tristam raised halfway out of his seat, then sank back with a frown. "That's impossible, Mama."

"Well, I'm sure I don't know," she said, picking up her needlework and setting a stitch. "It has been many years since I heard the story, and at the time I thought that the explanation was much too complicated and unreasonable. I should not be a bit surprised if it were all a hum."

He put a hand to his forehead and rubbed it thoughtfully. "What about the 'dark doings at Colter Abbey'? Rowan tried to tell me something, and I was under the impression that it somehow concerned ducks."

"Indeed? Let me think." She set two more stitches, then put down her embroidery again. "Nothing comes to mind, but there is something amiss, it would seem. At least I have heard my friends speculating on why Regina does not bring the girl out. She was an exquisite little child, you know, and would be the most beautiful girl imaginable if everything were right with her. Perhaps she is ill."

Tristam shook his head.

"No, not ill?" his mother continued. "But years

ago—perhaps it was only one or two, actually—we were taking tea with Seffronia—now let me remember who was there. Ah, yes, it was Emily Cowper and Isabella Bellamy. Emily said something about little Callie's 'indisposition.' Seffronia became quite upset, I remember. Her face grew pink, and she said that children often had such problems, but outgrew them. And she added, quite hotly I remember, that the old queen of Spain suffered from the same complaint, but none of her children inherited it."

They looked solemnly into each other's troubled faces. "From what did the old queen of Spain suffer?" Gracia asked her son.

"She had a dashed long horsy face," he observed, "but that's not the problem in this case."

Gracia's eyes widened with alarm. "My darling!" she cried. "You are not developing a tendre for this poor afflicted creature!"

"Of course not!" he said, reassuring her quickly. "It is only that she is the sister of my best friend, and while I was at Colter Abbey Rowan Dillworth began prating to me of ducks, or some such nonsense."

"Ducks?"

He waved a hand. "Something of the sort." Suddenly he let out an exclamation of satisfaction. "Ah! I have it! Webbed feet. There's a rumor that Miss Belcroft has webbed feet."

Gracia shook her head. "I think not. If there had been any sort of physical deformity, Seffronia should certainly have confided in me when the child was born. She'd have turned to me for comfort."

"Then it's all nonsense," he said, rising and stretching his long limbs.

"Well . . ." Gracia began. "If only I could be sure. Is there something else, perhaps? Rumors of erratic behavior? The old French king was known as Charles the Mad, you know. He had a deplorable habit of running about over the rooftops at night, shouting down chimneys to frighten lovers in their beds."

Tristam laughed.

Gracia smiled reluctantly. "He was also known as Charles the Beloved, however, so I collect he was not evil or dangerous in any way."

"Indeed," he agreed. "And I'll wager these rumors about the Belcroft girl, whatever they are, are without foundation—merely the result of envy or some such thing. Regina and Osgood have always been much admired; it is to be expected that a certain amount of envy would be engendered by so much charm and good fortune."

"Quite probably," she concurred. "But I beg of you, my love, avoid this girl's company until I can investigate more thoroughly. It will be very simple for me to ascertain the truth from dear Seffronia. And it would be the most dreadful thing if you were tempted to fall in love with someone who had tainted blood."

"Mama!" he protested. "How should I even meet her at this time of year? I certainly have no intention of running off to Colter Abbey again—or to anywhere else, for that matter."

But when, after dinner, a messenger arrived with

a letter from Brandy, Tristam broke open the seal and impatiently pored over its contents.

"Dear Tris," it said. "I have taken my sister to town, in hopes of entertaining her. Although the Season is past, there are many amusing things to take up our time. Please join us, if you can, as your company would make our stay much more enjoyable. Your obedient . . . Brandy."

After reading through the letter a second time, he spoke to his valet and within twenty minutes had mounted his fastest hack and set off for London.

The morning after the Belcrofts' arrival in town Lord Tristam presented himself at an early hour. Brandy had not yet made an appearance, but Lady Regina was seated at the breakfast table, sipping a cup of steaming tea.

"Ah, sir," she exclaimed, "please do come in and join me."

"I am too early," he apologized.

"No, no, I assure you! I can think of nothing more delightful than having a refreshing little chat with a friend over a cup of tea—or coffee, if you would prefer it. Such a happy way to start a day."

Tristam smiled and accepted the seat she indicated with a graceful gesture of her hand. As she poured out a cup of tea for him, Brandy ambled into the room, rubbing the tip of his nose with the back of a hand. He paused in the doorway to yawn broadly. Then he caught sight of his friend.

"Ah, Tris!" he exclaimed with pleasure. "Did you ride or drive?"

"I rode."

"Excellent! You shall go for a turn about the park with me. I must take some vigorous exercise to wake myself up."

"Certainly," Tristam agreed.

"And you are planning to spend a few days in town? You must come to a party we are planning for my sister. I wish you to become acquainted with her."

Tristam brightened visibly. "I should be delighted."

As Brandy sank onto a chair and accepted a cup of tea from his mother, Lord Osgood strode into the room. A heavy scowl was distorting his handsome features. He drew up sharply at the sight of Tristam and for a moment stood in the doorway, hesitating. Then he smiled pleasantly.

"My dear," he said warmly to his wife, "I find myself with mountains of paper work to attend to. Please send my breakfast to the library when it is properly prepared."

"Certainly, my love," she told him with a dazzling smile. "But do not drive yourself unnecessarily. You deserve a bit of relaxation after the killing hours you have endured at the abbey these past weeks."

Osgood's smile stiffened, but after a glance at Tristam, he broadened it and bowed graciously to his wife. "I shall attempt to regulate my zeal. A good day to you all." And turning crisply on his heel, he strode out of the room.

"Mama," Brandy chided, "shame on you for teasing him so. Everyone knows he has not lifted a finger these past weeks and has been hounded incessantly by his steward."

But she was holding up a finger, urging them to silence. All three listened to the sound of Osgood's retreating footsteps. Suddenly a fierce scowl contorted her ladyship's lovely brow.

"I knew it!" she spat. "He has left the door open between the yellow drawing room and the blue. He does it incessantly, to pique me. Excuse me . . ."

She hurried out of the room, and a moment later there was the sound of a door being slammed shut with horrendous force. Brandy sighed. Scowling furiously, Regina reappeared and seated herself stiffly in her chair.

"I shall have that door nailed shut!"

"Please," her son protested, "is it such a serious matter? Can you not overlook it? I am confident he would soon desist if you would pretend it was of no consequence."

"Impossible!" she said. "It *is* of consequence! Only last May that odious Madame de Reaux pushed her way into the house when Rimpson distinctly told her that I was not at home; he put her in the blue drawing room, and she sat listening to every word we said while Lady Whittington and I dissected her reputation, neither of us realizing that the door had been left ajar into the yellow saloon. Disreputable creature! And she has caused me nothing but discomfort since then, spreading the most dreadful rumors about me—all completely false, of course."

Brandy chuckled. "I am confident no one takes them seriously, no matter what they might be."

"But they do! You know how eager the ton is to ridicule. Why, you've no idea the strange way people look at me—some actually appear to be afraid. And it was only with the greatest difficulty that I was able to ascertain her perfidy. She has been telling the world that we are mad."

"What!" Brandy exclaimed. "Is that possible?"

Regina nodded. "She has told everyone that she knew the Valois family in France and that the madness which gripped poor old King Charles VI lies latent to this day in his descendants, often surfacing unexpectedly in violent outbursts and manifesting itself in various forms of eccentricity. There are in London at this time, thanks to Madame de Reaux, any number of weak-minded persons who will not stand within twenty feet of me for more than a few seconds, for fear I shall suddenly go berserk and do them bodily harm."

Brandy leaned back in his chair and laughed merrily. "What do they expect you to do? Certainly a small, gentle woman like yourself is capable of doing no very great damage."

"You do not understand," she explained. "A mad person is supposedly imbued with enormous strength. These fainthearts expect me to attack savagely and leave a path of corpses strewn in my wake."

Brandy laughed again; but as he looked at his mother's troubled countenance, he sobered.

"It's ridiculous. Even old King Charles the Mad did not resort to physical violence during his lapses.

Aunt Seffronia explained that he was a remarkably gentle creature."

Regina nodded. "That is true. But the word *mad* conjures up every sort of terror in the weak-minded."

Brandy turned to his friend. "Have you heard any of these nonsensical rumors, Tris?"

Tristam set down his cup and looked off into space, a slight flush rising to his cheeks. "I refuse to listen to gossip," he explained. "I consider it to be one of the most destructive forces in the universe."

"You are right, of course," Brandy agreed.

"Indeed, indeed," Lady Regina said, rising from her chair. "More harm is done by gossip than by all the remaining evils of society combined." She sighed. "Now I shall leave you to attend to my correspondence. Expect an invitation to our party, Lord Tristam; and enjoy your ride in the park." With a smile and a nod toward them both she swept out of the room.

Chapter 5

Tristam and Brandy were descending the front steps when a comfortable old barouche drew up and stopped. It was occupied by a handsome woman of indeterminate age whose garments, while of recent design and excellent quality, were not the latest kick of fashion.

"Aunt Seffronia!" Brandy cried. "How do you manage to resemble a fresh breath of spring when it is already the middle of August?"

Miss Valois put the tips of her gloved fingers over her lips and let out a ripple of delicious laughter, then stood on tiptoe and kissed Brandy's cheek.

"My dearest child!" she gurgled. "I am so delighted you have come to town." Turning to smile at his companion, she extended her hand. "And Tristam, my dear. How is your mama?"

"Well enough, ma'am," he told her. "Considering."

"Yes, yes," she said, quickly assuming a solemn expression. "She is adjusting to the loss of your father, poor darling. We should think of a pretext on which we can bring her to London. She would recover so much more quickly with her friends gathered around her for support.",

"I shall urge her, ma'am."

She patted his hand. "Such a dear boy." She turned back to her nephew. "And how is *your* mama, my love?"

Brandy grimaced. "She and my father are as usual; and their disagreements are aggravating every situation." He cocked an eye at her and gave her a speaking look.

"Yes, yes," she said, shaking her head unhappily. "I can imagine the problems which are created by their constant squabbles. Well, I shall see what I can accomplish. Look in on me later at Upper Grosvenor. We shall discuss our strategy for solving this dilemma."

"Now, my dears," Seffronia announced, seating herself in a businesslike way on one of the library's deep leather sofas, "we shall have a council of war. Council of love, I should call it, I realize; but the important thing is that we must agree on the steps we shall take to introduce Callie comfortably into the ton, and on the stories we shall circulate. I, for one, am in favor of admitting to everyone that she walks in her sleep."

Cries of protest rose from both Regina and Osgood, but Seffronia raised a hand to silence them.

"No, no, please hear me out. I have discovered that somehow rumors of her affliction have reached the world, and because the truth of the matter has been concealed, the ton has fabricated its own de-

tails. One rumor came to my ears some time ago—
that Callie has webbed feet. Such an infamous accu-
sation! I was appalled. Of course I denied it vehemently. I said, 'She is perfect in every way—a
goddess.' "

Regina nodded with satisfaction. "Excellent, my
dear. You did precisely the right thing."

"Yes," Seffronia agreed, "but immediately they
began to fabricate other tales. One friend confided to
me—only after prolonged pressure, I might add—
that there is a rumor Callie has a bizarre birthmark
on her right thigh. It is supposedly shaped like a
perfect crown and establishes her as the only true
heir to the throne of France."

"Nonsense," Osgood protested. "The Valois line
went out of power over two hundred years ago.
There was never any doubt about the right of the
Bourbons to succeed."

"That is what I explained," Seffronia told him.
"But my friend went on at some length, spinning out
the most preposterous faradiddle, and despite my
knowledge to the contrary, I nearly believed her myself. When Society is determined to gossip, it will do
so, come what may, and there is no stopping them
with such ineffectual devices as logic and good
sense."

Regina began to stride back and forth across the
floor, musing. "Then you suggest, my dearest Seffronia, that we should put up a sort of smoke screen
to hide the truth, is that right? Put forth rumors of
a minor and harmless affliction to draw attention
from the true one? We could say, for example, that

she suffers from an aversion to cats—perhaps even faints at the sight of one, or finds her breathing affected by their fur."

"No, no, no!" Seffronia exclaimed. "I am suggesting that we tell the truth. If we lie, we shall certainly be caught out; and walking in one's sleep is not such a serious malady, after all—certainly not like having webbed feet or a birthmark which might imply other characteristics inherited from a mad king. I fear that we have accomplished infinitely more harm than good by concealing this innocent foible. Remember Walter Scott's lines from *Marmion*—the ones which deal with deception."

Regina and Osgood looked at each other blankly.

" 'Oh, what a tangled web we weave,' " she quoted, " 'when first we practise to deceive!' We have made matters worse by being secretive—as though we were ashamed of this insignificant, minor complaint."

"But I am ashamed of it!" Regina exclaimed, tossing her head. "If the ton were to find out, we should be the laughing stock of England."

Seffronia sighed. "Well, if I cannot coax you into telling the truth, then we must resort to other tactics, I fear. As reluctant as I am to do so, I suggest that we adopt the ruse you proposed—that is, put out another rumor which will lure Society away from the others—the one about cats, perhaps."

"No, that will not accomplish our purpose," Osgood said, shaking his head. "Society will cling to the rumors it has already devised—which are much more intriguing, you must admit. The only solution is to find a willing young husband for Callie and get her off our hands as quickly as possible."

"Will anyone marry a girl who may walk out a window to her death at any moment?" Regina asked her husband scornfully. "I doubt it."

Osgood chuckled. "He may be delighted to be rid of her before many years have passed."

"Heartless!" Regina cried, scowling at him.

His eyes narrowed. "And, of course, you are the epitome of kindness and consideration!"

She glared. "While we are speaking of consideration, sir . . ."

Seffronia leaped to her feet. "Stop! Both of you! I came here today in an effort to help this unfortunate child. But one thing I must make clear to you—you shall stop this incessant quarreling, or I shall wash my hands of you once and for all."

Regina planted her hands on her hips. "Indeed, Seffronia? What leads you to believe that you can dictate my behavior or Osgood's?"

"You have requested my assistance in launching Callie properly and arranging a proper match for her," Seffronia pointed out stiffly. "It is impossible for me to do so if you continue to make yourselves figures of ridicule."

"Ridicule!" Regina cried. "I cannot believe it! You are taking liberties with the truth in order to make your point."

Seffronia was trembling. "I assure you, my dear sister, that I have never in my life taken liberties with the truth. There are as many nonsensical stories about you circulating among the ton as there are

61

about Callie. It is said that your reason and Osgood's are in question."

Momentarily struck dumb, Regina opened her mouth and wagged her jaw furiously at Seffronia. Before she could find her tongue, Osgood raised a hand and said gently to his wife, "Please, my dear, do not distrust your sister. I have heard these rumors myself, presented to me in a playful manner by many of my acquaintances—the source of many a good chuckle. But now, as Seffronia suggests, we must make an effort to present a picture of such amiable respectability that everyone will consider us the veriest bores; the tattle mongers will weary of us and pass on to fresh victims."

"Well," Regina said slowly, "that may be. It will not be necessary to maintain the pretense forever."

"And who knows?" he said, casting an urbane smile in her direction. "By the time Callie is married, a new understanding may have been reached between us. Imagine my bliss if I could boast of a docile wife."

Regina laughed shrilly. "Indeed not, my dear! You should find such a wife tiresome beyond measure."

"Perhaps," he agreed. He turned to his sister-in-law. "With our cooperation, Seffy, do you see your way clear to rescuing the girl?"

"I do indeed!" she told them. "I have given the problem much consideration, and I am now of the opinion that, without much difficulty, we shall succeed in luring that kindly, charming, and delightfully rich young man, Rowan Dillworth, to the altar."

* * *

Shortly after noon at another house in Grosvenor Square Rowan Dillworth settled himself in front of three soft buttered eggs and a steaming cup of coffee.

"Foster?" he said.

"Yes, sir?" his man replied, pouring coffee into his cup and adding precisely the proper-sized dollop of cream.

"My friend, Brandon Belcroft, has a sister."

"Yes, sir."

"And there are rumors about her, are there not?"

Foster assumed a tragic face. "Yes, sir. I am grieved to say that there are."

Rowan lifted a warm, flaky brioche from a basket and broke it apart with his fingers. "What precisely are those rumors?"

"Not that I credit them myself, sir," Foster hastened to assure him. "Most uncharitable rumors."

Rowan frowned. "Yes, of course. But what are they?"

Foster cleared his throat. "Among other things, sir, it is said that she has three breasts."

Rowan dropped the pieces of his brioche. "Three breasts! Good God! I have never heard such nonsense!"

"No, sir," Foster agreed. "Spurious rumor, I have no doubt."

"Dashed vicious gossips! Will say anything to destroy a reputation." Rowan picked up a piece of brioche and stuffed it into his mouth. "I could perhaps have accepted the story of webbed feet, but three breasts! Brandy should take someone to task for spreading such slander."

"Yes, sir," Foster agreed.

There was a silence while Rowan munched at his breakfast.

"So what is the truth, man? Where did all these insidious stories begin?"

Foster cleared his throat. "I fear, sir, that the truth is"—he hesitated a moment for dramatic effect—"the truth is that Miss Belcroft is mad. Being descended from the mad French king—her being a Valois, you see."

Rowan pulled another brioche out of the basket and broke off a piece. "You can't be sure of that. It's only a rumor like the others."

"No, sir, I regret to say that it has been confirmed by many of my colleagues. It is the reason her family keeps her locked away out of sight at Colter Abbey.

Rowan moved his fork back and forth impatiently among his egg yolks, drawing the outline of a crown upon the white porcelain plate.

"My friend Brandy is also a Valois, and he has never displayed the slightest sign of madness."

"No, sir," Foster agreed. "Most certainly not."

"And Miss Seffronia Valois, his aunt, is a Valois. There could not be a more level-headed lady."

"No, sir," Foster nodded. "A most intelligent lady, indeed."

"And Lady Regina Belcroft is a Valois," Rowan continued. He stopped as his thoughts raced back to the scene in the breakfast room at Colter Abbey. "Hmmm . . ." he said thoughtfully.

Foster was discreetly silent. Rowan sighed. Setting down his fork, he rose to his feet.

"I shall pay a call on my friend Belcroft. No doubt he is wondering why I did not appear last night." One corner of his mouth pulled back in a wry smile. "I should like to ascertain for myself whether or not Miss Belcroft has three breasts; but I have no doubt she will be shut away out of sight, as usual."

Rowan's confidence, however, was misplaced. When he was ushered into Belcroft House a short time later, he found Lady Regina bending over her needlework frame in a small withdrawing room; and after she had greeted him warmly and he had kissed her hand, she gestured toward a pair of open french windows, saying, "Brandy is in the garden. Do, please, join him there. He wishes to present you to his sister."

"His sister!" Rowan exclaimed, starting violently. "Miss Carolyn Belcroft?"

"Yes," she said with a smile. "His *only* sister."

For a moment he hesitated.

"Please," she urged.

Taking a fortifying breath, he strode to the windows. There he paused again for a moment and discovered, to his surprise, that his heart was beating faster than usual. Giving himself a little shake, he stepped out into the sunshine.

The sight which greeted him was not the sort which would ordinarily have caused alarm. On the lower terrace Brandy was strolling slowly away from him with a slender, graceful young lady on his arm. When they reached the end of the walk and turned back toward him, Rowan's breath caught in his throat.

Carolyn Belcroft was, without doubt, the most beautiful girl he had ever seen. Framing a delicate fairy face, she had piles of finely spun golden hair which made him think of windswept meadows filled with buttercups; and she wore an expression of such acute apprehension, that he felt himself drawn to her immediately.

"Ah, here you are at last!" Brandy called. He turned to smile at his sister. "Here he is, my dear, just as I predicted."

Callié smiled slowly, her lips parting slightly to reveal a row of even white teeth. Rowan had just turned his attention to her bosom and was inspecting it when he realized that she was extending a hand to him. Bending over it quickly, he pressed her soft fingers to his lips.

"We are planning some excursions for my sister's entertainment," Brandy told him. "I have suggested the Tower, as a beginning, and you must accompany us. Were you not saying only last week that you've been hoping to visit the Tower since you were a small boy?"

"Yes, indeed!" Rowan agreed, his eyes brightening. "I have promised myself that I shall not let another season pass without viewing the menagerie there. In the old days it was necessary that I be the most abominable nip-farthing; but the moment I came into a few extra groats, I promised myself I should indulge all my boyhood fancies. I also mean to view the Elgin Marbles."

Callie turned shining eyes on her brother. "It would be such a delight to see the Elgin Marbles. Aunt Seffronia was speaking of them just this morning, and she said that they still have the dust of ancient Greece upon them. So romantic!"

"You shall see them," he assured her. "Indeed you shall!"

Rowan, his eyes fixed on Callie's lovely face, continued, "And there is one advantage to being in town at this time of year: Bartholomew Fair will be in session next week. Not just the permanent shops which are in Smithfield the year round, but the extra stalls and attractions which are brought in for the fair itself. It's a delightful hurly-burly sort of place, I am told. And I have promised myself that I shall take a ride on the famous Ups and Downs."

Callie clasped her hands. "Ups and Downs? What manner of contrivance is that? May we take such a ride, Brandy?"

"Certainly," he agreed. "I visited Bartholomew Fair with Uncle Edward when I was seven years old, and a more delightful day I have rarely spent. Most exciting—riffraff galore—mountebanks, gypsies, charlatans of every kind. Plus all sorts of remarkable sights." He turned to smile at his sister. "Tristam and I were speaking of the place only this morning, and he is eager to accompany us. With Rowan and Tris and I in attendance, you may be assured that you shall be safe, no matter what evils we encounter."

"I am confident I shall be," she assured him.

They strolled the length of the terrace to a spot

where a stone bench had been placed under a shade tree. After seating Callie, Brandy sank down beside her and leaned his back against the trunk. Rowan settled himself on a large flat boulder opposite them, from which vantage point he could cast surreptitious glances at Callie's bosom without being detected. Bestowing a gracious smile on their guest, Callie turned to her brother in time to see his eyelids drop comfortably closed. A soft purring sound emanated from his nose.

"Brandy!" she cried. "You're not going to go to sleep! You must join in the conversation!"

"What?" he said, stiffening. "The conversation? Yes, yes, of course!" He cleared his throat. "What conversation?"

"We were speaking of Bartholomew Fair," she reminded him.

"Of course," he agreed. "Bartholomew Fair. Delightful place. We must go there." At which point his eyelids began to sag again.

"Brandy!"

With a supreme effort he roused himself. "Let me see," he said, his eyes roving blindly from side to side. They focused on Dillworth, and he brightened.

"Ah," he said. "Rowan must tell you about Meadowmere. He is doing remarkable things there—putting in a reflecting pool which will rival that at Versailles, and he is contemplating the construction of a ruined chapel."

Callie smiled. "A ruined chapel? How does one build a ruin, Mr. Dillworth?"

"Ah," Rowan said, warming quickly to his subject, "that is the most intriguing thing, Miss Belcroft! It must be placed in such a way that it peeps through a shrubbery. And we shall plant ferns and bracken among the stones—also, for construction, we shall select blocks with moss already established on them. Actually, it will require a bit of time to mellow completely, but it will be remarkably convincing from the very first, I am assured."

Callie laughed softly. "How clever of you to think of such a thing."

"No, no," he protested, his face glowing pink with pleasure. "I have hired the Prince Regent's architect to create all these amazing things for me. I am not a bit clever. In fact, I am the most thickheaded gudgeon in the entire realm."

"That is not true," she chided. "Brandy has often told me what an extremely clever person you are." She turned to her brother. "Is that not true, Brandy?"

Their only answer was a gentle rumbling sound. She grasped him by the shoulder and gave him a vigorous shake. "Brandy!"

"No!" he cried, sitting up with a start. "What is it?"

"You've been asleep, you odious creature!"

"Certainly not! Wide awake!"

"Then what has Mr. Dillworth been saying?" she asked, turning with a shy conspiratorial smile toward Rowan.

Brandy grinned. "He was telling you about Meadowmere."

Rowan let out a bark of laughter. "You have the

wits of a poacher, my lad. Of course I was talking about Meadowmere. Do I ever speak of anything else these days?"

"It's a subject which is of interest to everyone," Brandy assured him. "We all like to imagine what we would do if we were suddenly endowed with enough brass to make unlimited improvements on the mansion of our choice. I can tell you truthfully—though I trust you'll never breathe a word of this to my father—there are a good many changes I'd make at Colter Abbey if an uncle of mine were to die and bequeath me half a million pounds."

Callie's eyes widened. "Half a million pounds! What an enormous sum!"

"Yes," Rowan agreed, chuckling happily. "A delightful sum, I assure you."

They sat smiling contentedly to themselves, each visualizing the advantages of vast wealth, until Brandy's eyes began to sink closed again.

"Monster!" Callie protested, giving him a shake.

Glancing at his watch, Rowan leaped to his feet. "Good heavens! It is nearly three o'clock, and I have an appointment with my architect at a quarter past. I must run." He bent over Callie's hand. "Your obedient servant, Miss Belcroft."

Brandy struggled to his feet. "Yes, yes, Ro. I shall speak to Tris about our excursions, and we shall make some plans which are convenient for all of us."

"Indeed yes!" Rowan agreed. "Let us arrange a trip to the Tower tomorrow, if he is free."

But late in the afternoon a note arrived from Lord

Tristam, and as Brandy perused it quickly, a frown furrowed his brow.

"He accepts the invitation to your party," he told Callie, "but he will be unable to accompany us to the Tower or the Elgin Marbles, as he has been called home to Marcourt—something to do with his mother. I hope she is not ill."

"I hope not, indeed," Callie agreed.

"But we shall await his return before we contemplate a visit to Bartholomew Fair. We wish to have as large a party of stalwarts as possible, to insure against mishap in that den of thieves."

Chapter 6

At Marcourt, Tristam sat in his study, poring over a set of documents which his mother had laid out for his consideration. He frowned.

"I see nothing here that is so urgent, ma'am. It all could have been dealt with in due course."

"But I had no idea when you would return," she pointed out, "and Mr. Widdows was most adamant. He said the matter must be decided before the first of June."

Tristam leaned on his elbows. "The first of June is nine and one-half months away."

Lady Gracia nibbled her lower lip and turned to walk slowly away from her son, trailing a finger along the top of a table. "You went off so suddenly, my love, and I did not know why. How could I know when you would return?"

"But nine and one-half months, Mama? I have never been away for more than a week or two at one time. I only wished to speak with my man of business in London."

"You usually summon him here," she reminded him.

His brow tightened. "I also wished to look at some cottages on my Ludland estate. Humber is urging me to effect some repairs to three of them, and I have not made up my mind whether or not it is necessary. I thought I would take care of both problems at once."

Lady Gracia turned to peer anxiously into his eyes. "You did not visit Callie Belcroft?"

Tristam smiled and shook his head. "I did not. What sort of maggot have you got in your brain?"

She shuddered. "The most terrible things! Elvira Marling came to tea today. She has known the Belcrofts since the year one, and she swears that the girl is mad. 'Mad as a hatter' were her words. The child is subject to sudden fits of insanity and runs screaming through the corridors of Colter Abbey—especially when the moon is full."

"Elvira Marling has witnessed this picturesque sight herself, I presume," Tristam observed, shutting his back teeth tightly together. "This is all firsthand information?"

"Well, no," Gracia admitted. "But her cousin, Maria Dunbridge, received the account from a young parlormaid who was once an under-kitchen-maid at Colter Abbey—so it must be true."

Tristam ground his teeth. "Must be true, indeed! More likely utter rubbish! And we shall not be a party to spreading such malicious slander!"

"But, my dearest, you will not pay court to the girl? Please promise me that you won't."

Tristam leaned back in his chair and shook his head solemnly. "Mama," he said, "if, at my age, it is necessary for you to direct my every move, then I fear that the Waivering fortunes are at a very low ebb. Let us hope that I have wits enough not to fall in love with a mad woman."

Gracia immediately fluttered to his side and wrapped her arms around him. "My dearest! Of course it is not necessary for me to guide you! Your judgment is excellent! It is only because I have heard these dreadful stories that I am behaving in this absurd manner." She put a hand distractedly to her brow. "I have always been so fond of dear Seffronia —poor unhappy creature, if any part of it is true."

The following days proved to be more of an ordeal for the entire Belcroft family than anyone had anticipated. Callie's first sortee into Society, a trip to Madame Antoine's to order a ball gown, was a chilling experience. No sooner had she entered the portals of that august establishment and been presented to Lady Cowper, one of Seffronia's bosom bows who was passing through town on her way north to visit some friends, than she became aware of certain muffled whispers in one corner of the room and discovered that a group of ladies had drawn into a cluster and were leaning their heads together, peering at her.

Callie's first reaction was shock and embarrassment. Then, rallying her forces, she told herself that she was imagining disapproval in their attitudes— that they were only watching her as they would examine any young lady, judging her gown, her hair, and her demeanor. But it quickly became apparent to her that these ladies were wearing expressions of marked constraint. There was a sense of withdrawal in their postures and a wariness in their stiffened smiles which could not be ignored. Later, when she recounted the episode to her mother and Brandy, Callie could not hold back the tears.

"They were mocking me," she wept. "Somehow they have found out that I walk in my sleep, and they were saying, 'There she is.' I nearly died of mortification, Mama. If Aunt Seffy had not held me firmly by the arm, I should have turned and fled."

"Well!" Regina snorted. "If they were mocking us, I shall find a way to make them sorry!"

"No, no, my love," Seffronia protested. "They were not whispering about sleepwalking. They were saying, 'What a beautiful girl!'" She patted Callie's arm. "For you are, my dearest, and you must believe me when I tell you it is true. They were saying, 'So fairylike in her jonquil merino walking dress with braided trim and Polish epaulettes'—that sort of thing."

Callie sniffled. "Then why were they opening their mouths in that horrified manner? And exchanging glances of marked alarm? I assure you, they were censuring me, and for what other reason could they do so but that I am afflicted in this odious way, and the fact is common knowledge?"

"Here, here," Brandy chided, sliding an arm around her shoulders and pressing a handkerchief into her hands as she broke into a fresh flood of tears. "You must not allow yourself to despair. Soon you shall have your party and be surrounded by all our particular friends. They will behave in a warm and wonderful manner, I assure you, and you'll discover how much affection can be found in Society. I am confident that every minute will be filled with pleasure for you. Bear in mind that you have promised a dance to Rowan Dillworth."

"But I collect he only asked me out of kindness," Callie mumbled. "I have noticed that he also watches me in the most peculiar way. I frequently find him staring at the front of my bodice. What does that mean, do you suppose?"

Regina and Seffronia exchanged glances.

"I cannot imagine," Brandy admitted. "But he has told me he considers you a delightful person. I am confident that you and he shall become the most excellent friends—and it is my fondest hope that you should."

Callie looked up at him in surprise. "Surely you do not mean to make a match between Rowan Dillworth and me!"

"And why should we not?" Regina asked, raising a hand. "Dear Rowan has asked me many particular questions about you, my dearest, which has led me to believe that he is developing a tendre for you. And I should be delighted to discover that it is true. What could be more comfortable than an alliance with such a kindly, charming, and enormously rich young man?"

Lady Regina stood in front of her pier glass, a picture of voluptuous perfection in cherry satin, her ebony locks swept into a mound of enticing curls and her glistening white teeth peeping from between rosy lips. She made a pretty little moue at her reflection.

"Ah, yes, Jureau," she said to her abigail, "this is quite satisfactory. It will be Callie's party, to be sure; but the members of Society who have seen fit to accept our invitations will realize that I am still a woman of some looks—a figure to be reckoned with in this age of shallow beauties and insipid fashions."

Jureau smiled. "Miss Callie is a very lovely young lady, to be sure; but she will never compare with your ladyship."

Regina nodded and resumed her seat at the dressing table. "If you will please secure my tiara."

Jureau had just put out a hand to pick up the elaborate piece of filigree when there was a heavy knock on the door. Regina stiffened for a moment. Finally she sighed. "We must see who it is, I suppose."

The abigail went quickly to the door, but before she could reach it, there was another forceful knocking, and the moment she had opened it a crack, Lord Osgood shoved it wide and strode into the room, clutching a small bouquet in his hands. His wife rose angrily to face him.

"Ah, my dear," he began, clucking uncomfortably. "You see that I have come to you on a peace mission." He held out the posey to her. "Really too absurd the way we've been squabbling these past few years. Never liked it above half. And we were such excellent friends in the beginning. What I mean is . . . well . . ." He paused and looked at her earnestly; then, as though seeing her for the first time, he exclaimed, "Good God, Regina, you're a beautiful woman!"

She stood staring at him for a moment, her mouth open. Then she tilted her head coquettishly and gave him her most charming smile. "My dearest! How delightful of you!"

"Here, my love," he said, shoving the posey into her hands. "Please wear this for me tonight. Shall we banish our little differences? So wonderful if we could bill and coo the way we were wont to do at the start."

With a radiant smile Regina closed her hands around the bouquet. "My dearest dear!" she murmured. "So kind! How marvelous indeed if we could recapture the past! Do you remember those heavenly days we spent at the duke's villa near Cannes before Brandy was born? Those exquisite evenings with the scent of orange blossoms—the moonlight on the sea. You were a prince of lovers."

"Ah, yes," he agreed, staring dreamily into space. "I remember the way you napped on the terrace every afternoon with your back against the laurel tree. The exquisite line of your arm and throat against the green of the shrubbery—I have never forgotten."

Regina raised the bouquet to her nose. "And the fragrance of these flowers recaptures the glory of those days, my darling. The aroma of daphne and citrus blossoms and . . ."

She looked down at the flowers in her hand and gave a violent start.

"Yellow? Osgood! I am wearing a cherry gown!

And the colors in the party rooms are pink and blue. This yellow bouquet will clash dreadfully. I cannot carry it."

"Cannot! Indeed you shock me! How inhuman you have become over the years! I have made an effort to please you, and you scorn it."

"Effort!" she cried with a trill of harsh laughter. "What *effort* have you exerted in the matter, pray? A simple question addressed to your valet, sir, would have sufficed to ascertain the color scheme for our festivities. Instead you present me with this disharmonious offering."

Lord Osgood was trembling. "Disharmonious, indeed! If it had been a disharmonious emerald necklace or something of enormous price instead of mere blossoms, you'd have been delighted to receive it, whatever colors you were wearing. In fact, you'd have deafened me with your squeals of delight and smothered me with slaverous kisses."

"Slaverous!" she shrieked. "You brute!"

"Shrew!" he shouted. "And to think I actually demeaned myself in an effort to bring harmony to this house."

Shaking with fury, he lunged at her dressing table. Both Regina and Jureau gasped and retreated in alarm. But instead of reaching for his wife, he snatched up her tiara, cocked an arm, and flung the shimmering confection with all his strength against the wall. It landed with a clunk in the corner, scattering small diamonds over the floor. Regina let out a stifled protest as he turned on his heel and marched out of the room, slamming the door with such force that the window frames rattled in sympathy.

For a moment, thoroughly stunned, Regina and Jureau stared at the damaged tiara. Then the abigail hurried over to pick it up and hold it out in front of her for inspection. She clicked her tongue.

"I fear it is quite ruined, ma'am, and diamonds all over the carpet. You'll not be able to wear it until it's been sent to the jeweler."

"Nonsense!" Regina snapped. Snatching it from the abigail's hand, she plopped it onto her head. "I shall wear it as it is, and if anyone should quiz me, I shall not hesitate to recount precisely what has occurred. If Osgood thinks he can mock me with yellow nosegays and smash my tiaras, he is sadly mistaken."

Jureau clicked her tongue again, but Regina, muttering darkly to herself, insisted that the abigail pin the ruined headgear in place on top of her elaborate coiffeur. When at last she was ready to descend to the public rooms, she stood in front of her pier glass and surveyed herself, still flushed with anger.

The tiara's topmost wreaths of diamonds leaned drunkenly to the side and showed gaping strips of metal where many of its brilliants had been lost; its lower band dipped rakishly over Regina's right eyebrow.

"Despicable man!" she pronounced. "Wicked, evil creature! I shall repay him for this! Where is the red dye I purchased last week?"

Jureau tilted her head to one side and stared down

at the floor, "I'm sure I don't know what you mean, ma'am."

"Of course you do, you silly girl," Regina snapped. "I am referring to the dye I meant to dribble onto his lordship's waistcoat."

Turning imploring eyes on her mistress, Jureau sank to one knee. "Please, your ladyship," she pleaded. "Forgive him tonight—for Miss Callie's sake."

Regina snorted. "This will in no way affect Miss Callie. I insist that you bring the dye to me immediately."

With a heavy sigh Jureau rose to her feet and opened a nearby cabinet. Rummaging in a back corner, she drew out a small bottle of deep-red liquid.

"Now," Regina said with satisfaction, "you shall procure my special little glass vial from the Tudor chest and substitute our white boutonniere for the one which is undoubtedly sitting in readiness on your master's dressing table." She giggled. "I cannot wait to see his face when he begins to receive his guests, and a mysterious excretion seeps down the front of his apple-green waistcoat."

Jureau fluttered her hands. "Please, m'lady! Don't ask me to creep into his lordship's dressing room. If he was to catch me, he'd turn me off on the spot."

Lady Regina was pensive for a moment. "That is true. I shall do it myself."

"But if you could forgive him just this one time," Jureau coaxed. "For Miss Callie's sake . . ."

"Well, I can't," Regina told her. "His affront to me has been altogether too barbarous." And sweep-

ing her skirt to one side with her foot, she marched
grandly out of the room.

Chapter 7

When Regina descended to the vestibule, she found Seffronia, the first to arrive, handing her cloak to Rimpson.

"Ah, Regina," she called happily, "how regal you look." Then she tilted her head to one side. "But what a strange tiara you are wearing. I must speak frankly, my dear, and tell you that it is not set on your head properly. It is all askew."

Regina snorted. "Thanks to my odious husband! In a fit of pique he dashed it against the wall and ruined it. However, I'll not allow myself to be intimidated. I shall wear it tonight, as I had planned, and send it tomorrow to be repaired."

"But my dearest," her sister pointed out, "the tip is slumped to one side in the most preposterous way, there are stones missing, and the right side dips down nearly to your eyebrow. Certainly your guests will note something amiss with it."

"Then I shall describe to them the full extent of Osgood's villainy!"

Seffronia fluttered her hands. "Please, Regina! You must not quarrel with Osgood tonight. I am aware that he can be most difficult at times, but for Callie's sake we must all exercise restraint."

Regina sniffed. "I have already exercised herculean restraint in not attacking that odious man with an ax." She tossed her head. "Say no more about it or I shall be obliged to become very cross with you, my dearest, and that I would deplore. Come, let me look at you. Such a lovely gown—ivory is the most becoming color of all."

Seffronia smoothed her skirt. "Yes, it is a fine silk, and I was obliged to consider before I bought it—it was frightfully dear. But it will serve me for several seasons, I am confident, and I have planned carefully so that its purchase will not be an undue strain on my resources. Of course, I shall not be able to have any other new gowns this year."

Regina nodded, fingering a puffed sleeve. "Excellent stuff. Come, let me show you what I've done with the party rooms; I'm delighted with the results."

She linked her arm through her sister's, and together the two ladies walked off in the direction of the ballroom.

After her experience at Madame Antoine's it was with a feeling of acute trepidation that Callie watched the clock hands march relentlessly toward the hour of her party. She was tempted to feign illness and had even begun to feel a real headache at the thought of greeting so many strangers, all of whom she knew would be peering at her intently, as though she were a specimen under a magnifying glass. When she complained to her mother, however —she had managed to effect what she considered to be a remarkably convincing pallor—her parent exclaimed indignantly, "Indeed! Whatever can you be thinking of, you foolish girl? You must greet your guests tonight whatever your condition—even if you are dying of a virulent fever."

Callie had, therefore, steeled herself and, garbed in a gown of heavenly blue and with her curls arranged à la Sappho, made her way down to join her mother and Aunt Seffronia at the head of the staircase.

"Ah, my love," Regina caroled, touching her daughter's shining head with a tender hand, "how pretty you look! You must smile your sweetest smile tonight and greet everyone with the utmost graciousness. And if anyone should peer at you in a peculiar manner—which I am confident they will not do— merely smile more brightly than ever, for there is no one in the entire world who is capable of presenting a more angelic picture than you, my darling, when you pull your lips back ever so slightly in that delightful way of yours and twinkle your eyes."

Callie considered this request and for several seconds tried to picture the exact expression her mother wished her to achieve. After arranging her lips in three different positions and experimenting with five eyebrow elevations, she at last allowed her features to settle into what she considered to be an appealing smile. But Lady Westham, the first guest to mount the stairs, glanced at her rather nervously, and her son, the Honorable Frederick, took her hand cautiously and raised it quickly to his lips, all the while watching her in an alert manner which implied a readiness to bolt if the necessity should arise.

They had no sooner passed toward the ballroom than Osgood joined his family, resplendent in pale-green waistcoat and white trousers. His gaze lingered momentarily on Regina's tiara, then quickly passed on to Callie, whom he gave a nod of approval. He raised his sister-in-law's fingers to his lips.

"Ah, Seffronia," he sighed, "such a beauty and always a soothing influence on everyone."

As he straightened up, Callie noted that there was a stain of red on his lapel. It was obvious to her that, although Seffronia's eyes were downcast coquettishly over her fan and she had not noticed the blotch, Regina was aware of the slowly widening color; but instead of pointing it out to her husband and laughing in her customary derisive manner, her mother merely smiled to herself and turned to greet the next group of guests.

These acquaintances appeared to be no more at ease than the first. A plump matron, a sandy-colored young lady with a face liberally strewn with freckles, and two dandified young gentlemen greeted Seffronia in strident, high-pitched voices, bowed with infinite courtesy toward Regina, then approached Callie warily. After they had moved on, she heard the matron whisper to one of the young men, "It is as we feared. Poor creature." But she was unable to determine whether the woman was referring to Regina with her lopsided tiara, her father with his stained waistcoat, or to herself.

She was trying to decide on a way to alert her

father to his disaster without drawing more attention to it when Rowan Dillworth came bounding up the steps and Callie felt a surge of relief.

"Yes, yes," he exclaimed, pumping Lord Osgood's hand up and down. "Delightful evening, sir! Lady Regina—never saw anyone so regal; Her Royal Highness could take a page from your book." He bowed over Seffronia's hand. "Enchanting, Miss Valois!" Then he turned to Callie and his mouth fell ajar. "Miss Belcroft! Dashed beautiful! Take one's breath away."

In her relief at being among friends at last Callie laughed delightedly. Two couples on the staircase hesitated at the sound of her voice and waited.

"Yes, yes," Rowan repeated. "Radiant, Miss Belcroft! Please remember your promise to dance with me."

"She'll allow you the first, if you wish it, sir," Regina told him, "as you are such a special friend to us all."

"Indeed!" he exclaimed, his face glowing with pleasure. "Honored, I assure you." He lifted Callie's fingers to his lips once more; then, with a barrage of additional chuckles, he proceeded happily on his way to the ballroom.

After his departure Callie was again obliged to force a smile to her lips. She was somewhat heartened to note, however, that each new arrival now found more to interest him in Osgood's waistcoat and Regina's tiara than in herself. It occurred to her that she would have been greatly cheered by the sight of Lord Tristam arriving in the vestibule below them, but he did not appear, and as the minutes wore on, she was obliged to accept the fact that he would probably not attend her party after all.

Eventually the majority of the evening's guests had passed into the ballroom and strains of incidental music emanated from that chamber, accompanied by a symphony of voices babbling in a variety of pitches. The Belcroft family left their place at the head of the staircase and made their way to join the others. It was at that moment that Osgood discovered the depredation to his waistcoat. By this time the stain had run all the way from his white boutonniere to his waist. He let out an exclamation of dismay, cast a fulminating glance at his wife, and bounded up the stairs to disappear into the upper reaches of the house. Tucking her lips together, Regina led the way into the ballroom.

In the doorway Callie hesitated, staring around the room in surprise. She had seen the decorations earlier in the day—the ribbons, the rosettes, the pink and blue blossoms banked on all sides exuding their fresh, sweet perfumes—but tonight, with the chandeliers ablaze and the music lifting everyone's spirits, a new dimension of pleasure had been added to the scene. She felt her face relax into a real smile. Then Rowan came bounding toward her, beaming with happy anticipation, and she reached out a hand to him.

"Yes, yes, Miss Belcroft," he purred. "We shall lead them off to an evening filled with delight."

At that moment the orchestra struck up the notes of the polonaise, and as the other dancers fell in behind them, their bright-hued silks and satins transforming the ballroom into a swirling kaleidoscope of color, Callie decided that the world was in reality a much more charming place than she had realized. The future was spreading bright and inviting ahead of her, and there was still the possibility that Lord Tristam would arrive before the ball was over. That, she was confident, would make her happiness complete.

During the polonaise Rowan made every effort to maintain a dignified mien and set a serious tone for the other dancers, but it was apparent that he was enjoying himself immensely, and he kept lapsing into chuckles and casting warm, encouraging glances at Callie. She found his humor contagious; before long she was also purring happily to herself. Then the polonaise drew to a close and she realized, with a pang, that she was about to be deprived of her partner's support. Turning to glance around the room in the hope that other smiling swains would be awaiting the opportunity to solicit her hand, she discovered to her dismay that she was staring into serried ranks of cold, forbidding faces. For a moment she was tempted to cling to Rowan's hand and keep him with her.

The music ended, and Dillworth stopped on the dance floor to chat amicably with her before delivering her to her next partner. As they talked, she became aware of a group of guests at one side of the room who were clustered around a singularly exquisite tulip, all hissing and growling at him while he bit his lip and scowled. For a time he kept shaking his head and muttering at them in the negative, but finally he raised his face and stared anxiously across the room at Callie. Then, blinking back a grim expression, he squared his shoulders and set off unsteadily toward her.

He was ten feet away when a lock of hair which had sprung loose from its bonds crept over Callie's right eye and began to tickle her forehead. She raised a hand to brush it back. Like a rabbit that has been flushed from a thicket, the young man immediately veered sharply to the left and scurried off into one of the salons where refreshments had been laid out. Rowan, who had been watching his approach, let out an exclamation of surprise.

"What's up with old Phillips, I wonder?" he muttered. "Dashed peculiar behavior, if you ask me. But Phillips always was a loose screw. He's off to procure a glass of wine, no doubt. Fallen victim to John Barleycorn, poor old chap."

Callie swallowed hard to depress a lump that was rising in her throat. Staring unhappily at the formidable array of hostile young gallants which lined the walls, she cast about frantically in her mind for an excuse to keep Rowan beside her. She was almost tempted to catch hold of his hand and cling to it. But before she could thus disgrace herself, a young man with a thoroughly intimidating, stony face stepped out of the crowd and made his way solemnly across the floor.

"Dashed if it isn't Westover coming to ask you to stand up with him for the country dance," Rowan scowled. "Arrogant sort of fellow, but a good dancer. Won't tread on your feet."

Westover stopped in front of them and, without appearing to bend anywhere, somehow managed to bow to Callie. His voice, she noted as he requested the honor of dancing with her, was as hard and metallic as his face.

Rowan gave her a reassuring smile and departed. Callie cast about frantically in her mind for something to say to this glacial young man, but before it was necessary for her to speak, the orchestra began the introduction for the first country dance, Westover held out a hand in her general direction, she placed her fingertips lightly on it, and he led her stiffly to their places.

During the ensuing set she watched him curiously out of the corner of one eye. It was apparent to her—as it was to everyone else who observed him— that his interest was far removed from the Belcroft ballroom, though he executed the steps without error. There were times when it was necessary for him to approach his partner, and this he did without looking at her, each time fixing his gaze on a far wall. Callie began to worry that they would miss each other as they passed, committing a hideous faux pas which would render them absurd in the eyes of the hostile assemblage. But they completed the dance without mishap.

So intense had been her concentration, however, that Callie found herself quite exhausted by the end of the set. It was with infinite relief that she saw Brandy and Rowan hurrying toward her. The two young men quickly whisked her away to one of the salons, where they procured a glass of lemonade and insisted that she drink enough to revive her. She raised the goblet to her lips and gratefully swallowed the cool liquid. After a few minutes her spirits began to rise again.

"See here, Callie," Brandy told her conspiratorially in an echoing stage whisper, "you must not encumber yourself with these sticks, like Westover, who has put you through such an ordeal. The man never smiles, and how any female can endure that gloomy face of his is more than I can fathom. You must say no, you are engaged, when another long-face approaches you. You'll not last through the evening unless you can somehow contrive to enjoy yourself." He glanced quickly around them. "Ah, there's Bembley. He's the jolliest rogue we have the pleasure of entertaining here tonight."

Before she could stop him, he strode off to collar his friend and drag him back to his sister's side. Bembley's eyes were flaring slightly as he approached, but he managed a stiff smile and bowed to Callie with a flourish.

"Miss Belcroft," he began in tones which were not altogether steady, "it would be a source of great pleasure to me if you would be so kind . . ."

"Yes, yes," Brandy assured him before Callie could plead an approaching headache, "she would be delighted, old chap. And try to cheer her up a bit. I fear this ball, with all its stiff-necked formality, is placing a devilish strain on her nerves."

Fortified with this ominous information, Bembley's smile froze completely. He hemmed for a moment.

"Well!" Brandy snapped. "Aren't you going to speak? Tell her about that chestnut of yours that outran Rattray's gray. You never seem to tire of that subject."

Callie turned unhappily away as Bembley mumbled something about ladies not wanting to hear nonsense about horses. He could not resist the subject for long, however, and was soon chatting happily with Rowan and Brandy, discussing the pros and cons of purchasing a racing mare which had recently come onto the market and deploring the "gypsy tactics" employed by a certain Lord Gramstoke when fobbing off his damaged stock. When the first strains of the waltz were heard, he dutifully left his friends, leading Callie onto the floor and into the most vigorous whirl of her life. For the next few minutes she was twirled and spun and swept between rotating walls and tiers of circling faces until she felt breathless and quite sick. As soon as the music stopped, it was necessary for Brandy and Rowan to rescue her again and ply her with lemonade before the room would settle back into place and her eyes straighten up in her head.

By this time Brandy was also beginning to watch his sister anxiously, but he passed her on to another dutiful guest, who treated her with such austere consideration that she felt herself moving close to tears. Through the silent maneuvers of a country dance she was able to glance toward the spectators from time to time and could see beyond any doubt that they were all observing her closely, many of them standing in little clusters whispering together and nodding their heads.

As the dance drew to an end, she beckoned to Brandy, and when they met at the far end of the room, she put a hand on his arm and leaned heavily against him.

"I am so weary," she told him. "I fear I must excuse myself and retire."

He sighed. "Indeed, this ball is not going as well as I had hoped. It never occurred to me that the ton would consider sleepwalking such a serious malady. How can all these people have heard rumors of it— for it is obvious that they have done so?"

"I must go to my room," she said.

"Yes, but not just yet," he told her. "It has been arranged that you and Rowan and I shall take Lady Aurora Grey to supper, and if you should cry off, I fear it would incite the worst sort of gossip. Besides, you will find the oyster puffs fortifying."

Before she could protest, Rowan came hurrying toward her, his face wreathed in smiles, and Brandy left them together while he went off in search of Lady Aurora.

Chapter 8

Callie would have preferred to sit with her friends at a small table some distance from her parents, but before she could alert Rowan to her wishes, he had steered her to a larger central board where the other Belcrofts were assembling, and had pulled out a chair and toppled her into it while he twittered happily over his shoulder at Seffronia.

"How delicious you look, dear lady," he chirped, settling himself in the seat beside her.

She tilted her head playfully and ran a hand over one of her sleeves, puffing it prettily with her fingers. "Dear boy," she murmured.

Smiling and gurgling, Rowan turned contentedly back to Callie. "Dear Miss Belcroft," he began, "perhaps you could see your way clear to giving me some advice on a new project I am considering for Meadowmere."

Across the round table from them Lord Osgood was directing his charm at the Marchioness of Holcomb, who was seated on his right. He had changed his green waistcoat for a pale-blue one, which somehow intensified the color of his eyes. In fact, it produced a sort of staring effect which Callie found unnerving, and she could not resist glancing back at him repeatedly, despite her efforts to give her full attention to Rowan. It was not long before she realized that her father was watching Regina in an unusually sharp, steady way, as though he were anticipating something.

His wife, her tiara still careening over one eye, had taken a seat a little way around the table from him and was dividing her time between vivacious conversation with her dinner partner, the Earl of Collingwood, and surreptitious glances at Osgood while she pretended to be unaware of his presence.

Callie could feel a decided tension in the air, and after a few moments she saw her father whisper to a footman, who then carried a glass of red wine to Regina's place and set it on the table in front of her while she was chatting with the guest on her right. A moment later Regina turned back to her plate, and eyeing the glass through narrowed lids, sent it down the table to be placed in front of Osgood while he was deep in conversation with the marchioness.

At that point Rowan demanded Callie's attention by asking her if she thought he should plant a maze at Meadowmere. While she was considering her answer, she observed that a new footman was again bearing the wine glass away from Osgood's place. But to her surprise he stopped behind Seffronia and set the glass in front of her. Immediately Osgood scowled and began to make vigorous hand signals toward the footman, who stood looking at him vacantly for a moment, then walked back to his master's chair to receive verbal instructions.

"Please forgive me, Miss Belcroft," Rowan pleaded, his voice thick with self-reproach. "Of course you are not interested in my Meadowmere. What a bore I must be to go prosing on about it all the time!"

"No, no!" she assured him. "It's a marvelous project. Only, I must consider a moment before I offer an opinion on such an important matter."

She quickly looked back toward her aunt in the hope that she could somehow prevent her touching the wineglass, only to discover to her horror that Seffronia had already raised the goblet to her lips, and a trickle of claret liquid was dripping out the bottom of the stem onto the front of her beautiful new ivory silk gown. As Callie watched, her hand over her mouth, Seffronia set the glass on the table, then stared down at the front of her dress in dismay. Her gaze went quickly to the glass, which was oozing from its bottom onto the tablecloth. Bewildered, she picked it up and examined its base. For a moment she sat breathing unevenly, then she slammed the goblet down on the table and rose stiffly to her feet, trembling with pent emotion.

"Oh!" she hissed through clenched jaws, glaring furiously at her sister, then at her brother-in-law. "You dreadful, *dreadful* people!" She rushed from the room, leaving a sea of bewildered faces behind her.

There was a long moment of shocked silence before Callie heard a woman behind her whisper,

"Have we done something horrid? Or is it possible that dear, gentle Seffronia too . . ."

It was some time before any degree of serenity could be reestablished in the supper room. Callie decided that the best course for her to take was to minimize the occurrence, and by stiffening her resolve, she managed to appear unmoved by her aunt's behavior, informing Rowan in her most confidential manner that she believed a maze would be an excellent thing to have at Meadowmere.

"They require infinite care and a great deal of time to mature before they are of use," she reminded him, "but I am convinced they are worth the effort."

Rowan was listening to her with only half an ear. "Is Miss Valois perhaps ill?" he asked.

"I think not," Callie told him. "My mother appeared to understand the difficulty, or she would have followed my aunt and made her comfortable."

"Yes," Rowan agreed, though in a distracted way; and he sat frowning to himself for some time before Callie was able to draw his thoughts back to his country house.

Brandy arrived a few minutes later with Lady Aurora Grey, and one look around the room was enough to bring a scowl to his face.

"Our parents have been up to their tricks," he observed, as he settled into a chair beside Callie.

She nodded grimly.

"I shall deal with them before the night is over," he muttered.

Callie sighed. "When may I slip away?" she asked him. "I really cannot endure much more."

"Perhaps after one more set," he suggested. "You do not wish to let it be bruited about that these gudgeons have driven you off with their staring and whispering."

Later, when the diners began to rise, Callie accompanied Rowan back to the ballroom; and when the music signaled the start of the minuet, she allowed Brandy to lead her onto the floor, where she went through the figures of the dance as prettily as anyone could have wished. But as soon as the music stopped, she put a hand on her brother's arm and told him in a low but determined voice that she must now depart, as her strength would surely not support her for even one more turn around the room.

"Very well," he agreed. "And I must compliment you on the fortitude you've shown, Cal. In the face of all this nonsense you've been a perfect brick."

She was smiling at him gratefully, relieved that the ordeal was at last to end, when a hush fell over the room. Everyone, she discovered, was staring at the entrance to the ballroom; and there in the doorway, a striking figure in black satin, his chin high as he gazed over the top of everyone's head, stood the Marquis of Waivering, quietly surveying the scene in front of him.

For a moment his eyes moved over the crowd, searching through the assembled gossips who were on one side of the room, then through the young blades who had collected in a cluster on the other. Finally he saw Brandy and Callie standing together, and he strode purposefully toward them, straight across the room. Glancing neither right nor left, he would have passed Lady Regina without seeing her if she had not stepped forward and planted herself firmly in his path.

"Ah!" she exclaimed, her voice tinkling with vivacity. "Tristam, my dear. So delighted that you were able to return in time for our little party."

He looked down at her curiously for a moment. Then, realizing who she was, he bowed over her hand.

"Good evening, ma'am. Please accept my apology for arriving at such an hour."

"Nonsense," she said. Locking her arm through his, she led him to the spot where Brandy and Callie were standing. "You have not yet made the acquaintance of my daughter."

Callie tipped back her head and looked up at him. She had not realized how remarkably tall he was; and as her eyes widened, he smiled and bent over her hand.

"An honor, Miss Belcroft," he said.

The orchestra was beginning to play again—this time a waltz. Tristam slid an arm around her waist and swung her out into the line of moving dancers. She felt a momentary qualm, remembering the furious ordeal to which Bembley had subjected her, but Tristam guided her easily, neither swinging her violently nor clutching her; and as they circled smoothly among the other couples, she felt a cool night breeze begin to flow in through the garden doors, brushing her cheeks, lifting her spirits, and sweeping her along on a cushion of cool, effervescent air. She looked up at him, her eyes wide and curious, and he smiled down at her. Suddenly she felt wonderfully refreshed and exhilarated, and before the dance had come to an end, her cheeks had acquired a delicious pink glow and her eyes were sparkling.

When the music stopped, Tristam would have led her away to a salon where wine and lemonade were still being served, but Brandy intercepted them and, before either could protest, presented her to young Viscount Starking. This stolid young man, who was rather plump and already unduly pink and damp from his exertions during the waltz, appeared to be no more pleased with this turn of events than Callie. But he dutifully requested her hand for the next set, and they took their places on the floor. During the ensuing country dance, which required an abundance of little jumping steps, the viscount suffered considerably. Callie tried not to watch his red-faced, earnest effort for fear she would begin to giggle. As the ordeal progressed, however, his labored breathing caused her more than a little alarm, and when at last the set concluded, she sent him off quickly in search of some sort of drink to refresh him. Before anyone else could solicit her hand, she fled into the shadows of some columns which framed the french windows and from their shelter began to peer around the room in search of Tristam.

He was nowhere in sight. She frowned to herself, wondering if he had perhaps left the ball immediately after making a brief appearance. If he had indeed departed, she told herself, she would retire to her room. Under no circumstances would she remain another moment in the ballroom unless there was a chance that she would have an opportunity to spend some time in his company—perhaps share a glass of wine with him and chat about the wonders they could expect to view on their excursion to Bartholomew Fair.

The room had grown unbearably hot during the country dance. With a quick glance around to be certain that she was not observed, she slipped through the windows onto the terrace. Outside, the night was cool and tranquil; and with a sigh of relief she took up a position in the shadows beyond the long shaft of light which fell through the window, fanning herself gently while she let the air wash over her hot cheeks. She could hear a group of women cackling stridently as they drew closer to the aperture.

"Dreadful!" one of them exclaimed, laughing brightly. "No hope for the poor thing, I'm told. And such a beauty! Imagine the conquests she could make if she were normal." She emitted a derisive giggle.

"It is obvious that the bad blood is on her mother's side," another voice observed. "Have you ever seen anything more absurd than Regina's posturing in that ridiculous tiara? And they say the ghastly smear on Osgood's coat was his wife's doing. I had thought he was bleeding from a wound that his demented daughter had inflicted." There were squeaks of laughter.

"Indeed!" the first woman chuckled. "And did you observe Waivering's fascination with the girl? Now we know what is required to hold the attention of that arrogant young blade—a face and figure of the utmost perfection, and a powerful streak of madness. Nothing less will suffice."

"I have been staring at the girl's bosom all night," the other chortled, "but I cannot determine if she has indeed three breasts."

Listening to this conversation, Callie felt her legs rapidly melting under her. In danger of immediate collapse, she fled down the garden steps, around the corner of the house, and into the sanctuary of a little conservatory which was attached to the rear of the mansion. There she sank onto a bench and allowed a flood of tears to burst forth. For several minutes she wept copiously, emptying herself of the terrible agitation which had built inside her during the long, tedious evening. When at last she had drained herself of emotion and was not able to sob out even one more droplet, she inhaled deeply and let out a long, shuddering sigh. It was only then that she became aware of another presence in the conservatory. Leaping to her feet, she turned in alarm to find Tristam standing a few feet away from her.

"Please," he urged, taking a step forward, "if there is any way in which I might be of assistance to you . . ."

She dashed the back of a hand across her eyes. "No, no, it is too kind of you; but it is all so dreadful! Have you heard the odious rumor which is circulating among the ton, sir?"

He solemnly shook his head.

"They say I suffer from a bizarre physical deformity, but it is false! Anyone can see at a glance that I have only what God intended." She held out her arms, inviting inspection of her silk-clad bosom.

Tristam surveyed her gently curving form, his cheeks taking on a faint glow. "Certainly, Miss Belcroft," he assured her, "there can be no doubt that He has bestowed perfection."

"And it is to Him I shall turn," she announced. "Life in this vale of tears is unbearable. I shall enter a nunnery."

"A nunnery!" he exclaimed. "How can you consider such a step! Only think of the sorrow it will cause your parents and friends."

Callie looked up at him miserably. "My parents would be happy to see me settled—even in a nunnery. And I must admit—though I know I should not speak in this manner—I would find it restful to be away from them. You have observed their pranks, I think. It is so distressing! I can no longer live this wretched life, always conscious that at any moment some dreadful calamity will certainly occur."

"But, Miss Belcroft, you must give the world an opportunity to win you over before you retreat from it."

"No," she said, staring grimly off into space. "I shall accompany my brother to Bartholomew Fair— that excursion promises to be delightfully entertaining—then I shall go into seclusion."

He rubbed a hand unhappily across his brow. "I shall speak to Brandy about this decision of yours. If we combine our efforts, we may dissuade you."

She shook her head and with a sigh settled onto the bench. Tristam sat down beside her. For a moment they were silent, then she looked up at him shyly.

"Have you ever been to Bartholomew Fair, sir?"

"Yes," he told her. "Several times. It's a rough-and-tumble place. You'll find it amusing."

Her expression began to clear. "Have you ridden on the Ups and Downs?"

"I have. It's a preposterous machine. You sit in an open box that's attached to the end of a long shaft. There are four of these shafts, like the spokes of a wheel, with a box on each end; and as the contraption turns, you rise in the air until you're quite high. Then, as you descend, your weight is used to counterbalance the other riders. It's a most entertaining experience."

Callie's lips parted in a faint smile. "I shall ride on this device, to be sure."

"Yes, you must," he agreed. "And you should pay a visit to the learned pig at the George Inn. I am aware that there is a trick involved, but he can add and subtract numbers and multiply fractions quite rapidly."

"That is most strange," she murmured.

As she sat quietly, contemplating a nearby potted plant, Tristam watched her appreciatively, observing the curve of her slim throat and the clusters of feathery ringlets that had collected around her ears and on the nape of her neck. When she turned back to him, he was smiling at her. She returned his smile, and for several seconds they sat in happy harmony, each allowing his thoughts free rein. Then the muffled strains of music in a new rhythm could be heard in the distance. Callie turned her head to listen.

"My brother is undoubtedly searching for me," she said, "hoping to send me capering about the ballroom in another ridiculous country dance."

"You would prefer to stroll through the garden?" he suggested.

She nodded. "I must confess, sir, that I should indeed. I have been weeping, and I fear that the damage done to my countenance would supply all manner of fresh fodder for the gossips, should they come to know of it." She leaned her face closer to his. "Is it still apparent that I have recently lost my composure?"

He peered deeply into her eyes, and for several seconds her question passed from his mind. Then he jerked himself back to reality and, pressing the tip of his tongue against the inside of his cheek, lied, "Yes, I fear so—just a bit. Let's walk for a time in the garden. The air is especially pleasant tonight, and there's a gentle, refreshing breeze."

She rose, and he rose beside her, drawing her hand through his arm. Guiding her out of the conservatory, Tristam led her down a shallow staircase and into the shadows of a shrubbery. For several minutes they strolled quietly, enjoying the cool flow of night air over their faces. They were both smiling contentedly as they rounded a corner of the garden path and found themselves facing the house. The blaze of lights which flared from the ballroom recalled Callie to herself.

"Sir," she asked, turning her face up to his, "is the

evidence of my recent self-indulgence still apparent?"

He studied her face, noting the soft blush of her lips and the thick, dark clusters of lashes against her cheeks. "Still a bit," he said, tightening his hold on her arm.

With a nod to each other they resumed their walk, both listening with pleasure to the sounds of the other's feet on the gravel and basking in the play of gentle air around them. At the corner, however, they came into full view of the house again, and as they paused to glance up at its graceful brickwork, a light flashed in one of Regina's bedroom windows. There was a splintering crash and a cry of protest. Callie began to tremble.

"Oh," she whispered, "they have started again."

Overwhelmed by compassion, Tristam guided her to a stone bench. There he urged her to sit down and sank onto the seat beside her. Immediately he was aware of the wonderful fragrance of her hair, which was close to his face, and the warmth of her slender body as she leaned against him. He was about to put his arms around her when Brandy came bounding down the steps from the house, striding rapidly toward them and calling, "Callie! Where are you?"

She leaped to her feet and rushed to him. "Oh, Brandy!" she cried, throwing her arms around his neck. "They are at it again. I heard the most dreadful crash."

"I know," he muttered. "No amount of argument can persuade them to end this lunacy. Aunt Seffy has washed her hands of them forever. She swears that she will never speak to either of them as long as she lives."

"What are we to do?"

"I don't know," he admitted. "I shall think it out when our guests have departed. In the meantime you must retire. I do not wish you to overtax your strength."

He turned to Tristam, who was walking up to them quietly.

"Ah, Tris," he said, "be sure to come to us tomorrow. I have things I wish to discuss with you, and we shall complete the plans for our visit to Bartholomew Fair."

Chapter 9

When Tristam arrived at Belcroft House the following day, he found Callie in the yellow saloon chatting happily with Brandy and Rowan Dillworth. Her cheeks flushed prettily at sight of him, and as she extended her hand to him, she gave him such a glowing smile that for several seconds there was a strident buzzing in his ears.

"We are discussing the time we shall visit Bartholomew Fair," Brandy told him, "and I had thought that tomorrow might be convenient."

"Yes, yes," Rowan concurred. "It would be a perfect time for me."

"Tomorrow would be excellent," Tristam agreed.

Callie clasped her hands together. "I can hardly wait. Will we see jugglers and puppet shows and mountebanks and all sorts of dancers?"

"I believe there will indeed be jugglers and puppet shows," Rowan observed. "And I've been told that there's a famous pieman there, a Mr. James Sharp England, who dresses himself as a tulip of the past century. We must purchase from him a piecrust pig with currant eyes."

Callie bounced up from her seat and began to walk restlessly in a circle. "After I have ridden on the Ups and Downs," she told the others, "I shall wish to attend a puppet show." She stopped and absentmindedly ran her fingers along the back of a chair.

Tristam nodded. "My cousin, Morgan Fenn, tells me there's an artist at the fair who performs a most remarkable motion. I have promised myself that I'll view it sometime."

"Indeed, sir?" Callie said. "We must certainly see this attraction." She dropped down on the sofa beside her brother and rested a hand on his arm. "What, pray tell, is a motion?"

"It is a little play," Brandy explained, "performed with dolls which are manipulated by wires. But Tris, if your cousin Fenn recommended it, I think it will not be the place to take my sister."

Tristam laughed. "That is true. It is probably not at all the thing for young ladies."

"One of us might attend the show," Rowan suggested, "and ascertain its nature—whether it is suitable for Miss Belcroft."

"Excellent!" Brandy agreed. He removed his sister's hand from his arm and examined it curiously. "What is this black stuff you have on your fingers, Cal?"

For a moment she looked at them in confusion; then her gaze shifted to the chair she had recently touched. "Oh!" she said. "It must be from that chair. But where on earth did it come from—such an ugly old thing? It is completely out of harmony with the other furniture in this room; and I cannot remember seeing it before."

Brandy sighed. "Lord Cavenleigh sent it around to my father. It's a chair which apparently belonged to old Lord Davenant Belcroft. The Cavenleigh family has had it in an unused room for over a hundred years, and the earl thought my father might like to have it."

Callie had risen and was examining the chair critically. "But do we want it?"

"Our father does. He was overjoyed to have it returned. Said, 'Now the set is complete,' whatever that means. I infer that he has several more like it at Colter Abbey, though I must confess I have never seen them."

"Nor I," Callie admitted. "They may be in one of the rooms in the north wing, which is never opened."

"It is possible," Brandy agreed. "I shall speak to the housekeeper and ask her why this one has not been cleaned. If it must remain in one of our public rooms, it should not soil people's clothing and hands." He took hold of the back and shook it vigorously. "At least it appears to be sound, despite its age. We need not fear an accident as the result of sitting on it."

He was wiping his hands with a handkerchief when the door opened and Aunt Seffronia floated in. She was wearing a white dress with a wide blue sash and cartwheel hat which lent a charmingly youthful air to her appearance.

"Aunt Seffy!" Callie exclaimed, hurrying to plant

a kiss on her cheek. "You have not washed your hands of us after all."

"Not of *you*, my darling!" she assured her. "I would never wash my hands of you! And I have decided to give your parents one more chance. But if they do not reform their behavior, I shall cease forever to acknowledge our relationship."

Realizing that the conversation was shifting to private matters, Tristam and Rowan quickly rose to bid the Belcrofts farewell. They bowed over both ladies' hands, agreed on a time for their meeting the following morning, and departed, descending the front steps together. As they reached the street, Rowan sighed heavily.

"Dashed fine-looking girl. Pity about the rest, what?"

"What *rest* would that be?" Tristam asked him.

"Her madness, I mean."

"Good God!" his companion exclaimed. "Surely you don't believe that nonsense. It must be obvious to anyone who has eyes in his head that she's as normal as you or I."

"Most of the time," Rowan agreed. "But she has fits, I am told—goes suddenly berserk for no apparent reason and runs screaming through the streets."

Tristam gave a snort of disdain. "I'll wager you've never seen her indulging in such antics."

"Well, no," he admitted.

"I thought not!"

"But I saw her capering across the roof one night."

"You cannot be sure of that, Dillworth!"

"Indeed I am! Brandy came out the window also

and tried to coax her back. I thought they were both going to fall to their deaths."

"Good God!" Tristam breathed. His voice had grown considerably weaker. "But you can't be positive."

"I *am* positive!" Rowan persisted. "She ran across the roof; and Brandy called all manner of strange things to her in order to lure her back to safety. He told her he was holding a kitten in his hands—which he was not. And he told her he had bought her a pony. Certainly a young lady her age would not have any use for a pony; why would he say such things if she were not reduced to childishness or some form of madness?"

Tristam stood frowning down at the cobblestones for some minutes. Finally he shook himself. "There is a rational explanation, I am confident."

Dillworth put a hand on his friend's arm and patted it clumsily. "The girl tipped me a settler too, old man, with that beautiful little face of hers and her charming ways. If it weren't for this other thing, I'd offer for her in a minute. But it's a hopeless situation, from what I hear." He shook his head unhappily. "There's more misery in this world than we can comprehend, Tris."

With a final gloomy nod he turned away and headed off down the street in the direction of his own house. Tristam stood watching him, his thoughts in turmoil.

For some time he remained where he was, scowling, musing, and arguing with himself. Finally he began to wander slowly along the street, still thinking deeply. He had not gone more than a few steps, however, before he discovered a familiar figure approaching—none other than his cousin, Morgan Fenn, his hat tilted jauntily over one eye and his neckcloth disarrayed. His nose, which was of a florid hue and intricately mottled, proclaimed his affection for John Barleycorn and, to Tristam's consternation, his rolling gait announced to the world that he was already in a state of gentle inebriation, despite the earliness of the hour.

"Ah, Tristam!" he caroled. "Just the man I hoped to see. You find me in reduced circumstances, old chap—not a feather to fly with. If I do not somehow dig up a monkey before dawn, I'll be carted off to Newgate."

Absentmindedly Tristam fished in his purse and pulled out a bill, which he handed to his cousin. "So, Morg," he observed, unhappily noting the premature flecks of gray in the man's hair and the unwholesome color of his skin, "the world's not treating you kindly these days?"

"Indeed not," Fenn admitted. "Monstrous cruel, in fact." He peered at his cousin through bloodshot eyes. "And methinks, from the look of that long-pulled-out face of yours, she's not treating you too kindly either."

Tristam bit at his lower lip. "Kindly enough. I've been with my friend, Brandon Belcroft."

"Ah." His cousin nodded, his face crumpling suddenly. "And with the pretty little changeling sister, I've no doubt. There, my boy, is a dreadful tragic tale." To Tristam's surprise several large tears appeared in his cousin's eyes and began to roll down his cheeks. "Here, here, old lad," he scolded himself, running the back of a hand across his nose, "there'll be none o' that, now. Cheer up! Cheer up!" He shook himself vigorously and, planting both hands on his hips, launched himself into a vigorous Irish jig, bounding in a circle around his cousin and singing in a strident tenor voice, "Oh, cheery me! Oh, cheery me!"

Tristam, his face flushing, glanced nervously around to see if they were being observed, then scrambled after him, grabbing for his shoulder. But Fenn danced out of his reach, singing lustily as the tears poured down his cheeks.

Suddenly he leaped into the air and clicked his heels together twice, landing with a clatter on the pavement and falling backward into a wrought-iron paling. Immediately righting himself, he leaped again, this time attempting to click his heels thrice; but he became entangled in his gaiters and came down in a crumpled heap on the ground.

"Good God!" Tristam exclaimed, picking him up and brushing him off. "Everyone is staring at us, you clodpoll!"

His cousin struck a pose and turned to peer around the square. The only figures visible were a nursemaid with her charge and a footman hurrying on an errand. Fenn bowed elaborately toward the nursemaid. The girl blushed and giggled behind a hand.

"Ah," he smiled, "an appreciative audience. It warms the cockles of me heart."

Tristam ground his teeth. "If you don't stop warming your cockles with blue ruin, you'll be in the basket before long."

"True," Fenn admitted. "But it's a happier way to go out of this world than with stark reality staring me in the face. Have you ever stopped to look around you, lad?" His eyes brimmed, and his mouth twisted into a miserable pucker. "It's a rotten world we live in!" With a sob he began jigging in place. "So I console meself as best I can."

He leaped into the air, this time managing to click his heels three times before he landed upright on the cobbles. "Ah!" he cried, brightening. "I did it! Old Grandfather Fenn could manage three clicks, even up to the date of his eightieth birthday. Do you remember that?"

"No," Tristam admitted. "It had slipped my mind."

"It has never slipped mine," Fenn told him. He jumped up again, but only managed one click before he landed off center and stumbled to one knee.

"Drat!" he exclaimed.

"Please, Morg," Tristam pleaded. "We're still within sight of Belcroft House. I'd never be able to face that family again if Brandy or someone came out just now and saw you flopping about in this ridiculous manner."

"Ah," Fenn sniffed, wagging a finger elaborately at him. "It would be better for you if you never faced them again. Flee from that crowd before it's too late, me boy. T'would be a dreadful thing for the Waiverings"—his lips trembled—"if our pride and joy was to take a fancy to the changeling girl."

Tristam bristled. "You know nothing of her, you bufflehead."

"I know that she has more than her share of pulchritude." Fenn grinned wetly. "Three of them, in fact."

He launched himself into another jig, but this time Tristam lunged at him and managed to catch him by the shoulder, giving his cousin such a savage shake that Fenn's hat flew off, spinning into the gutter and rolling for some distance before it came to rest against a chunk of dubious matter. Jerking himself free, Fenn picked up his beaver and wiped it tenderly on his sleeve.

"Monstrous bully!"

"Then behave yourself! It's damned irresponsible to spread such lies. I know for a fact that she does not have three breasts."

"Ho, ho!" Fenn chirped. "You *know*, do you? You're getting more proficient with the lasses than I had dared to hope. I'll be spreading the word that my cousin's not such a slow-top as we feared." He began dancing vigorously backward, waving his hat playfully in Waivering's face. With an impatient grunt Tristam turned away from him and stalked off down the street. Fenn capered after him.

"Don't let your heart triumph over your head, old man," he sniffled. "Charming though the chit may be, she's"—he swept off his hat and pulled his hair up on end, bulging his eyes grotesquely—"she's dicked in the nob." He burst into tears.

Tristam's self-control collapsed. "You damn fool!" he snapped. "Your antics are past enduring!"

"I know," Fenn bubbled. "I'm a shiftless sot, not worth a groat. I should leave the country and stop burdening my family."

"No, no," Tristam protested. "You're an ass, to be sure; but we're all devilish fond of you. Always have been."

Fenn sagged against Tristam's shoulder, rubbing a sleeve across his eyes. "Always thought you were, laddie. Can't resist the old elfin charm, what?"

Nodding, Tristam helped him to a seat on a mounting block, but as soon as he had settled him comfortably, he strode quickly away. Behind him he could hear Fenn's quavering voice rising in a squeaky, "Cheery me . . . oh, cheery me!" As he reached the corner, there was a squeal of protest from the center of the square, and glancing back over his shoulder, he caught a glimpse of the red-faced nursemaid in Fenn's arms being bounced over the cobbles in a rude facsimile of a country dance.

Chapter 10

That night Tristam did not sleep well. All manner of horrible dreams assailed him. Once he found himself wandering among a crowd of lunatics in Bedlam Hospital. To his surprise Brandy and Rowan appeared among the inmates, clad in hideous rags and moaning piteously. At sight of Tristam they both broke into Irish jigs and cavorted playfully around him; but when he tried to speak with them, they pulled their hair up into ridiculous tufts on top of their heads and rolled their eyes at him. Eventually they faded away. Then he found himself strolling along a stone passageway where maniacs were groveling on the cobbled floor, and rounding a corner, to his amazement, he discovered his mother chained to a wall, her face haggard, her eyes rimmed with dark circles. She held out her hands and wailed, "Oh, Tristam, help me, dearest! They say I suffer from a bizarre physical deformity, but I have only what God intended!"

Tristam stepped quickly toward her, but a fresh wave of madmen poured into the room, sweeping him backward. He found himself reduced to half his normal size and struggling frantically to escape the surging mob. Throwing out his arms, he shouted, "Help!" Instantly he was back in his own bed, hopelessly entangled in the blankets.

"Yes, sir?" his valet cried, hurrying into the room. "Your lordship called?"

Tristam groaned. "Get me out of this chaos, Jennings. The bedclothes are conspiring against me. That corner of the sheet is over here, and this one is over there."

"Indeed yes, sir," the valet agreed. "Everything is at sixes and sevens."

With a few deft movements Jennings managed to extricate his master from his bonds, and Tristam slid his feet out onto the floor. The sun was flooding the room with golden light.

"Well," he said, listening to a happy chittering of bird calls in the trees outside, "it's not such a wretched morning as I had anticipated."

"No, sir," Jennings agreed. "Indeed not. I should say it's a delightful morning for your lordship's visit to Bartholomew Fair."

As soon as Tristam had risen to his feet, he applied himself to the task of readying himself for the day and presenting himself at Belcroft House precisely at the appointed hour; but by some strange chance he executed his preparations with such dispatch that when he arrived in Grosvenor Square, a maid was still on the front steps of the mansion scrubbing the marble risers with a heavy brush. He turned away from her quickly and strode off down the street, around a corner, and along another thoroughfare, where he hoped he would not be observed by any of his friends' families or attendants.

As he walked briskly along, trying to decide how to occupy his time until it was expedient to present himself again, he looked around. To his surprise there was a remarkable amount of activity on the streets. Greengrocers with bags of produce on their shoulders hurried past; a covey of undergrooms rode out from the Belcroft stables and headed their mounts toward a back roadway where they could exercise the baron's horses; a glazier's assistant with a large plate of glass strode along the street in the direction of Rowan Dillworth's house while the glazier himself walked ahead, shaking a stick at pedestrians and opening a safe path for the transportation of his merchandise. All the artisans and merchants bowed ceremoniously to Tristam as he passed them.

It was not long before he found that he had proceeded in a circle and was again within sight of Belcroft House. Glancing at his watch, he noted that only a few minutes had elapsed since he had checked it last and he was still half an hour before the appointed time. He drew up at the edge of the square and stopped; and as he stared glumly around himself, watching with growing impatience the apparently aimless bustle and activity—hurrying footmen, gaggles of nursemaids scurrying along behind their charges' perambulators, tradesmen of every sort bearing burdens to the service entrances of the various mansions—he became slowly aware that he was suffering a strange turbulence in his humors. His phlegm was warring with his choler, or something of the sort, for he felt a restlessness—an irritability—which was foreign to his nature. He had a sudden vision of his cousin's tearstained face chanting, "Dicked in the nob!" and it occurred to him that he should make his excuses to Brandy and retreat posthaste to the safety of Marcourt, where he could hide himself away on a repairing lease until he was feeling more the thing. But then his mind conjured up a vivid picture of Callie's face looking at him with shining eyes while she held out her arms and said, "Anyone can see that I have . . ." And a pleasant warmth trickled over him.

As he was thus musing, the front door of Belcroft House opened and Rimpson came down the front steps. Tristam strode eagerly to meet him.

"If your lordship pleases," the butler began, "Lady Regina would be exceedingly gratified if you would take a cup of tea with her—if your lordship is not otherwise engaged, that is."

"Why certainly," he said, feeling a pleasant surge of anticipation. He followed Rimpson quickly into the house.

To his delight he found Callie seated with her mother, the two ladies considering a pile of envelopes which they were sorting and sticking into cubbyholes in a small secretary. Callie gave him a glorious smile of welcome.

He beamed back at her, aware that he was grinning in a thoroughly fatuous manner, but unable to control his face. Out of the corner of his eye he saw Lady Regina begin to extend her hand, hesitate while she stared at him in surprise, then continue to proffer her soft jeweled fingers as she called to him in a tinkly voice, "Ah, dear Tristam, such a pleasure to see you this morning."

With the greatest effort he drew his eyes away from Callie's radiant face and bent over the baroness's hand.

"Good morning, ma'am," he said. "We have perfect weather for our Bartholomew Fair outing."

"Yes," Regina agreed. "But I am concerned that it may become quite warm before the day is over." She turned toward her daughter. "My dear, you must promise me that you will come home at once if you feel the least bit oppressed. You must promise me that."

"Yes, Mama, of course I will," Callie assured her, casting a shy glance toward Tristam.

"And if you get the least bit weary, my darling, you must stop your activities immediately and come home to rest. Under no circumstances can we have you falling into a decline while you are in town."

Callie's face flushed slightly with embarrassment. "Be assured, Mama, I shall coddle myself as though I were the most delicate creature in the world."

Lady Regina squeezed out a brittle little laugh and turned to Tristam. "You must take her in charge, dear sir. Do not allow her to overtax herself. For example, she must partake of a morsel of food from time to time. You must all do so, in fact, to prevent fainting. One can do oneself irreparable injury by allowing oneself to become hungry on a very warm day. I am told that it can bring on fainting spells and even induce permanent softening of the brain."

Callie's brow knitted at these words, and she said to her mother with a hint of crossness in her voice, "How can one have softening of the brain when it is already the nature of the organ to be quite soft?"

Glancing shyly toward Tristam out of the corner of her eye to ascertain the impact her statement had made on him, she was startled to find him watching her in a singularly penetrating manner. It was the first time she had seen him near at hand in the full light of day, and she was delighted to discover that his eyes were even larger and darker than she had realized.

"Yes, yes," Brandy exclaimed, coming into the room so suddenly that even Lady Regina jumped. "We must remember to eat regularly and keep ourselves cool, and do all the things which will make our excursion more enjoyable." He turned to his sister. "How are you today, Cal?"

She scowled at him. "I am well, of course, as usual."

"Excellent," he said. "Then it is just a matter of awaiting the arrival of our other wayfarer before we can be off."

It was not many minutes before Rowan hurried into the room, puffing slightly and mopping his brow with a handkerchief.

"Dash it all, Brandy!" he complained. "Was it necessary to set such an early hour? And after all my scurrying about to ready myself I should not be surprised to learn that you have decided not to risk such an excursion today; not too safe to venture out among the masses when they're in this sort of ugly mood."

His host stared at him. "Mood? What are you talking about?"

"The Peterloo thing yesterday. Understand there are rumblings among the working people all over the country—claim the attack on Hunt and his crowd was completely unprovoked. Dashed chaotic sort of situation, from what I gather."

"But what's it all about?"

"The riot in Manchester yesterday," Rowan explained.

"I've heard nothing of it," Brandy admitted.

"Indeed? Henry Hunt led that bunch of his to some sort of gathering, and the local yeomanry plus the 15th Hussars were obliged to bring them under control."

"Then that's settled," Brandy pointed out. "Whatever their crimes, they were brought under control, which is undoubtedly why we've heard nothing."

"Heard nothing?" Rowan exclaimed. He turned to Tristam. "You either, Tris?"

"No," Tristam admitted. "And I have mills not far from Manchester; I should have been informed by now if anything serious had happened to them."

"Yes, yes," Rowan agreed. "That is true."

Lady Regina was looking anxiously at her daughter. "But do you think it's quite safe to subject Callie to the danger, Brandy, my love?"

"Mama!" Callie exploded. "They have just decided that there is no danger. And even if there were, I should never be such a paltry creature that I should be afraid to go about among my fellow countrymen. Let it be understood that I have never been accused of cowardice."

"Certainly not!" Brandy agreed. "We must not allow ourselves to be intimidated by every little rustle in the shrubbery. Where would England be today if her citizens had always been of such faint heart?"

Rowan was nodding to himself. "I dare say it's all a hum. If you two chaps have heard nothing . . ."

"Excellent!" Lady Regina said, rising and moving toward the door. "Then I shall be happy to have Callie occupied for the rest of the day while I tend to some important business."

Callie looked at her in surprise. "I had thought you intended to buy some new bonnets today, Mama."

"I do, I do," she assured her. "That is the very business to which I refer."

Chapter 11

During the trip to Smithfield Callie found it difficult to sit quietly in the barouche.

"How much farther is it, Brandy?" she asked every few seconds, and "What shall we do first? Should we look for the motion? Or should we ride the Ups and Downs the moment we arrive? Perhaps that is the best. Or shall we find Mr. England and eat a piecrust pig? Strangely I am suddenly quite hungry. Aunt Seffy told me she has heard that the black puddings sold at Bartholomew Fair are also quite tasty. What is a black pudding, pray?"

"Sounds devilish unpalatable," Rowan observed.

"I believe it is made from blood," Tristam told them.

"How dreadful!" Callie exclaimed. "Then I shall pass it by. But I shall be most eager to see one of the dumbshows. Is it really possible to play out an entire story without saying a word? If the Ups and Downs is in action, I think I should like to ride on that first, before anything else. Lord Tristam, would you be not averse to escorting me on the Ups and Downs, as you have ridden it before and can give me expert advice on precisely the way I should sit and hold my hands in order to prevent mishap."

"Indeed, I should be highly gratified if you would allow me to accompany you," Tristam assured her.

Brandy chuckled. "What sort of danger do you anticipate on that silly device, Cal?"

The girl looked at him curiously. "Is it not dangerous?"

"Certainly not! If it were, I should not allow you near it."

Callie's brows knitted slightly. "Then why should anyone wish to ride on it? I assumed that there was danger, which in turn would impart a marvelous sense of peril."

Brandy shook his head. "It is only to raise one higher and allow one to view the surrounding countryside unobstructed."

"But why can one not view the surrounding countryside from the upstairs window of a house?" Callie asked him.

"Perhaps," Rowan suggested, "it is the illusion of being unsupported which constitutes the allure of the Ups and Downs."

They were discussing this possibility when they arrived at the fair. Callie, moving eagerly about in the carriage to obtain a better view of the place, began to make excited sounds in her throat.

"It is even more thrilling than I had imagined," she told her brother, grasping one of his wrists and giving it an ecstatic shake. "Had you any notion it would be so crowded, Brandy? Did you realize that it was such an enormous field full of tents and booths and banners and such? And there on the side, those stone buildings with shops and inns—do they build them up each year especially for the fair? Is that the top of the Ups and Downs? I had no idea the boxes rose so high—like riding on a mill wheel, I should imagine, though I have never done so and cannot compare the sensations. Why are we stopping alongside this building? Look at the painting on the wall there, Lord Tristam. It is the learned pig you were speaking about. Brandy, we must certainly witness this pig's remarkable feats."

"Yes, yes," Brandy assured her. "We shall indulge ourselves in every possible fancy."

Callie tried to suppress a squeal of excitement. "Look there! The man in the satin waistcoat and powdered wig must certainly be Mr. James Sharp England. What is he carrying on his tray? It does not appear to be piecrust pigs."

"I believe it is hot plum pudding," Brandy observed. "Would you care to have a slice?"

"I should like it above all things," she assured him.

Brandy leaped down from the barouche and hurried off into the crowd. The two other young gentlemen had alit and were helping Callie to the ground when he returned with four slices of steaming dark cake and presented a piece to each of his companions. Callie eagerly took a bite, then looked at her brother in surprise.

"It is rather tasteless," she said.

He nodded. "Let us pass our slices on to a few of these urchins who are standing about. They may find it more to their liking." He distributed the puddings to four filthy little boys who were standing nearby. To their chagrin the ragamuffins were immediately set upon by four larger street arabs and deprived of their bounty. Brandy shouted at the aggressors and waved his arms, but all eight boys took flight and darted into the crowd, disappearing around the corner of a stone building. With a shout Brandy bounded after them. Callie and Rowan also shouted protests and followed in Brandy's wake. Tristam, more leisurely in his movement, required a moment longer to launch his large frame into action, and by the time he began to stride after his companions, they had all disappeared around the corner.

On the other side Brandy, Callie, and Rowan were obliged to draw up sharply to avoid crashing into the back of a crowd which had gathered around a tiny stage on which a seedy old man with no front teeth and only a portion of a right ear was putting two dirty white dogs through a series of tricks. The eight little boys had disappeared completely, but they had evidently been observed by certain members of the masses, for a wiry little man with a singularly unpleasant smile bared his teeth at Brandy and chirped to his neighbors, "Well, will you look 'ere, chums; flash morts on the trail of poor 'ard-workin' lads!"

Several other members of the crowd turned hostile faces toward them and drew ominously together in a cluster. Brandy, drawing to a halt, looked around in consternation while Callie leaned against his back and clutched the tail of his coat between her fingers. Rowan made clucking sounds in his throat.

"Give 'em a proper welcome!" the unpleasant little man continued. "Let these 'ere oppressors know . . ."

But his voice broke suddenly, and his eyes flared as he stared beyond Brandy. His friends goggled in the same manner and shrank away. Turning around quickly, Callie found Tristam striding into view, his head and shoulders rising high above the crowd.

"Cooo!" one of the hostiles exclaimed. When Callie turned back, she discovered that the wiry little man and his associates had miraculously disappeared, while those who remained were now presenting their backs and intently fixing their attention on the performing dogs. Brandy chuckled softly. Callie stepped quickly over to Tristam's side and slipped her arm through his.

He smiled down at her. "Shall we make our way through that passage over there and out into the field?" he suggested.

Brandy and Rowan nodded. The four friends pushed their way through the crowd and into a narrow cobbled passage which led between two stout beam-and-plaster buildings. A moment later they came out the other side, into the field where a dazzling array of pavilions and brightly colored booths were arranged in uneven rows. Banners of every color fluttered in the air, and a general hum of activity, overshadowed by a faint cloud of dust, cast a glow over the entire scene. It made Callie think of bees and honey and warm summer days with the fragrance of grasses being harvested; except that in this case it was also the odor of onions cooking, and spices, and hordes of unwashed bodies.

Brandy, who had stopped at the entrance to a large yellow tent, gestured to them. "This way," he called. "I have obtained four seats for the next performance, which is about to begin. The owner assured me that it will in no way offend the sensibilities of a delicately reared young lady."

"Ah," Rowan said with satisfaction, "it is Bramblestoke's Puppets. I have heard a great many favorable reports about them. I can guarantee, Miss Belcroft, that you will enjoy a most educational experience."

The puppet show proved to be more educational than Rowan had anticipated. At several points during the performance, while Callie watched wide-eyed and with lips parted, Brandy and Tristam exchanged uneasy glances and rose to remove the girl from the premises. But each time her innocent, fixed expression reassured them that the more pithy dialogue was passing over her head.

The artists had selected the tale of Lady Godiva for their play, and she was depicted as suffering from an acute hypermammillary condition, her globular breasts swelling luxuriantly over the top of her bodice. Peeping Tom had been elevated to a costarring role and was a wizened old puppet with a remarkably lifelike, lecherous face. He followed constantly in the lady's wake, endeavoring to pinch her derriere, but was repeatedly though inadvertently foiled by Lady Godiva's unconscious movements. He finally cackled lasciviously and evoked wild hoots of laughter from the coarser members of the audience by informing her with a wink and a leer that he would will his entire fortune to her if she would make it possible for him to tell his friends that he had *dug* his grave with his teeth. She replied smartly—in a startlingly masculine voice—that she had no "hintention" of *teat*ering on the brink of ruin; and she gave him such an expert rap with her fist that he flew offstage and was not seen again.

She next confronted Lord Godiva in his private quarters. He was found to be gamboling with several other busty females and at the same time quaffing from a jeweled chalice and belching resonantly.

"Sir," she informed him, "you are *owert*axing the people. Stop this 'ideous oppression at once!"

He laughed rudely and told her that he would never do so, " 'till ye rides *nekked* through the streets, me gel."

"You're a rotten bugger!" she told him; and the curtain fell.

It opened again almost immediately to reveal her ladyship gloriously nude and with her hair inexpertly draped about her in an effort to conceal her curves. She was mounted on a horse which strongly resembled a cow and which wore an even more lecherous leer than Peeping Tom had done. It kept swinging its rump suggestively while it winked one eye at the audience. The lady, riding across the stage, waved a fist threateningly at the exterior wall of a castle. Suddenly a window popped open and Lord Godiva put his head out, registered proper amazement, and scattered a handful of coins onto the pavement below. Accompanied by a roar of approval from the audience, the triumphant lady rode nonchalantly off, bowing repeatedly in a manner which threatened to reveal all her secrets to the world but never quite did so. She finally slipped from view, giving her admirers one last come-hither smile over her shoulder. Callie nodded with satisfaction. Leaning her head close to Brandy's, she expressed the opinion that Lady Godiva possessed a great deal of spirit and deserved to be commended.

After they had left the puppet show, Brandy, Tristam, and Rowan had a quick huddled conference and determined to scout out their entertainments in advance to prevent a repetition of the recent deplorable event. Rowan was deputized to investigate the propriety of the rope dancers while Brandy peeped into a nearby dumbshow, and Tristam, with Callie on his arm, walked leisurely over to the Ups and Downs to join the large crowd which surrounded that remarkable machine.

There was a considerable amount of bustle at the base of the contraption as an enormous fat woman with three tiers of bouncing chins serried all the way down into the front of her bodice was jammed into one of the boxes, her rolls of flesh pushed first to one side then another until the door could be shut upon her. Immediately she began to squeal with happy excitement and wave her arms.

"Good heavens!" Callie exclaimed. "Do you collect it will bear her weight?"

"I am confident it will," Tristam assured her. "Come along, we'll take a ride also. When Brandy and Rowan find us, we'll be up on the top of the flight and can wave down at them."

Callie drew back momentarily. "But this machine appears to be exceedingly fragile."

He smiled. "It is meant to appear so. Therein lies the thrill of riding on it."

"Very well," she said with a sigh. "I cannot allow cowardice to deprive me of adventure."

As they moved closer, the Ups and Downs let out a stentorian groan of protest and began to move, raising the fat woman inch by inch. She squealed giddily and jiggled in her seat. Immediately the machine trembled to a halt. The crowd caught its breath. After several anxious moments the apparatus shivered to life again and began to move, shuddering from time to time, but doggedly lifting its prodigious burden. In the crowd alongside Callie an emaciated woman in a cherry-strewn bonnet was bouncing wildly from one foot to the other and wringing her hands.

The fat woman was halfway up and the crossbar level when there was another ominous creaking from the wood. Unconcerned, she leaned over the edge of her box and called down to her emaciated friend, "Hoo, hoo, Zipporah, my dear, look at me. Is it not the most thrilling thing!"

Zipporah, her face white, whinnied through her teeth. Callie turned an anxious face toward Tristam, but he appeared to be unconcerned and, after paying several pennies for admission, helped her into the box which was at the bottom of the circle. Climbing in beside her, he pulled the door shut and waited for the attendant to fasten it on the outside. Callie clutched at his sleeve.

"Look," she breathed, "we are in the box which is on the opposite end of the shaft from the fat lady's. Is it possible that your weight and hers may place a fatal strain on this poor contrivance?"

He laughed. "I hope my weight will never be the problem to me that hers is to her."

"No, no," she said quickly. "Certainly not. Your weight is perfect." She broke off in confusion and for a moment gnawed on her lower lip as she tried to think of something diverting to say, but before she could sort out her thoughts, there was a fresh groan from the machine and it slowly began to move again. Forgetting everything but the perils of the ride ahead of her, Callie gripped Tristam's fingers and kneaded them anxiously between hers.

"Oh," she squeaked. "Oh, dear!"

By looking up she could see the bottom of the fat woman's box descending. On the ground the spectators were pointing up and laughing among themselves. Momentarily forgetting propriety, Callie leaned against Tristam and, closing her eyes, pressed her face against the front of his shoulder. There was a moment of silence as the box rose over the top of the circle and the creaking ceased. Then they began to descend. Callie turned her face slightly and peeked out of the corner of one eye. Immediately she forgot her plight and drew away from her companion exclaiming, "Oh! What a marvelous sight, is it not?"

"It is, indeed," he agreed. "I believe we can see every tent and booth from here. There is Bramblestoke's Puppets beyond the bright-red tent with the yellow faces painted around the top."

"Such color and bustle," Callie exclaimed, clasping her hands together. "And now that we know there is no danger . . ."

But at that moment, as their box descended, balancing the fat woman on one side and Tristam's considerable weight on the other, there was a horrendous moan of agony from the machine. On the ground Callie saw several spectators clap their hands over their mouths; all the faces peering up at them were suddenly wearing expressions of horror. Zipporah, whose bonnet had fallen over one eye, her cherries bobbing wildly, was staggering backward and forward sobbing, "Maudie! Great God in heaven, dearest Maudie!"

Callie clutched at her companion, there was a sharp cracking sound, and their box plummeted to earth.

Chapter 12

For a terrifying moment Tristam held her pressed hard against him. Then they landed with a thump. Wild screams rose from the other side of the machine.

"Are you hurt?" Tristam asked her in a tense whisper.

"No," she admitted, shaking herself. "Not a bit."

A ring of anxious faces was watching them over the rim of the box.

"Are you all right, sir?" a bystander asked Tristam.

"Yes, thank you," he told him. "I believe we are unharmed."

The bystander quickly unfastened the latch on the outside of the door and pulled it open. Stepping out, Tristam lifted Callie to the ground. Immediately the crowd's interest shifted to the other victim, who was ululating shrilly. Her voice rose and fell so penetratingly that many of the spectators had placed their hands over their ears and were falling back. When the operator, whose ordeal had already been considerable, could stand it no longer, he shouted, "Stop that squallin', ye daft old banshee!"

Instantly the crowd turned on him.

"Wretch!" a goodwife cried. "Hurlin' poor wictims about wi' no thought o' their safety! Nobody cares for the innocents no more."

"Such a monstrous contraption!" a youth shouted.

"Inwention o' the devil!" another yelled.

Callie tucked a hand into Tristam's and leaned against him. "Why are they so angry?" she whispered. The marquis shook his head indulgently.

Holding her tightly by the hand, he guided her around the machine to the spot where Maudie was still wedged in her box, keening piteously, her mouth hanging open and her eyes rolled back in her head. Zipporah was trotting distractedly back and forth in front of her, wringing her hands and sobbing, "Oh, dear God! The poor darling!"

Tristam cleared his throat. "Here, now, my good woman," he said to Maudie in a firm, resonant voice, "give me your hand and we shall see if any harm has been done."

Maudie stopped shrieking and brought her eyes to focus on the marquis. "Oh," she said in a sweet, small voice. "Have I been injured, your lordship?"

"That we shall soon ascertain," he told her, unfastening the latch on her box. "Give me your hand and I'll assist you."

With a pretty smile and coquettish bob of her head she extended a plump white hand. He took it and pulled. The crowd waited expectantly, nodding and

139

smiling, but the woman remained wedged fast in the box. After Tristam had tugged several times to no avail, a sinewy young farmer, smelling richly of mountain byres, burgeoning grasses, and pig droppings, climbed onto the beam and shoved as Tristam pulled. Three concentrated efforts were required, but eventually they managed to haul Maudie to her feet. Tristam handed her gallantly to the ground. She stood for a moment staring around curiously at the crowd, as though she were surprised to find herself in such company. Zipporah, throwing her arms around the woman's neck, began to blubber.

"You're not hurt, Maudie? You got nothin' broke?"

"I think not," Maudie observed. "I appear to have had a miraculous escape."

"Miraculous escape!" the operator snorted. "Nobody never got 'urt on the Ups and Downs."

There was an ominous rumble from the crowd.

" 'Ow many times it come down, I'd like to know?" a voice shouted. Several members of the crowd surged onto the broken beam.

"Never!" the operator yelled, his face fiery with anger. "An' you stay back over there! Don't you go 'armin' this amazin' device! It be the property o' Mr. Jonas B. Darkwater, who'll 'ave yer 'ide if they's any damage done. I be tellin' you, an' it be so!"

"Oh, it is, is it?" roared a large ragged man with a purple face. "The same Mr. Jonas B. Darkwater, no doubt, what preys on workin' folks and don't give a hoot if their wives an' childer be killt! Burn the damn thing down; then it won't 'arm nobody else!"

"No!" the operator shrieked. "Get back, I say!"

But the crowd had begun to seethe around the machine, and several husky men were already dragging chairs and tables away from a nearby black-pudding stand to pile against the contraption. A woman in a greasy black dress and with a look of savage determination on her face was snatching piles of tracts from a nearby stand and dumping them onto the pyre while the owner raced after her shouting, "Stop! You can't do that!"

An instant later someone struck a flame to the pile and it leaped up in a flash, sending a column of thick, black smoke soaring skyward.

"Get the operator," a spectator shouted. "Throw him on!"

There was a skirmish on the other side of the machine. When the participants sorted themselves out, the operator had disappeared. Tristam, his arm around Callie's shoulder, backed away from the searing heat. Someone behind them screamed, "Water! Get water!"

The flames were spreading with alarming speed and quickly engulfed the entire machine, leaping off the top box, high into the sky. At its base the frenzied crowd ran in every direction, dragging chairs and tables from inside an inn. Callie turned to one side and discovered to her amazement that vandals were pulling down all the nearby tents and booths, adding them to the conflagration. She watched a group of men run out of Bramblestoke's with their arms full of puppets. Immediately they began to toss them onto the flames. They were carrying several versions of Lady Godiva in various stages of dress and undress; one of them was the naked lady who had concluded the performance. To Callie's surprise the doll appeared to be permanently fused to her horse.

"Stop!" she cried, leaving Tristam's side and plunging into the melee to tussle with one of the vandals. "You can't wantonly destroy these little creatures!"

But the malefactors dumped their booty onto the bonfire and ran off in search of further mischief. Callie found herself unexpectedly in possession of the mounted lady, which she was clutching by one of the horse's hind legs.

"Is it not the most dreadful thing?" she said to Tristam, who had come up beside her. "All these people running about in this lawless manner?"

"Yes," he agreed. "We are inside a mob and must make every effort to escape. There is no telling what will happen when a mob is on the rampage—especially today, when their mood is so ugly. They may take a sudden dislike to your bonnet or to my waistcoat and throw us onto the fire with the puppets and black puddings. We shall try to press through in that direction." He pointed over her shoulder. "As I remember, we are near the passage where we entered. When we're on the other side of these buildings, we'll find a safe place to wait for Brandy and Rowan. They are undoubtedly searching for us in the midst of all this confusion."

Callie and Tristam drew together and by leaning into the crowd managed to move a few steps. But it was not long before the mob tightened, and despite their efforts to move the other way, they were driven backward toward the fire. Clinging desperately to her companion's hand and clutching Lady Godiva to her breast, Callie let out a stifled protest. "We're going to be burned, sir!"

Tristam struggled against the force of the mob. By leaning hard into that relentless stream he managed to plant his feet, but by that time he and Callie had been driven so close to the blaze that the girl was obliged to shield her face with the puppet.

"Stop!" Tristam commanded the crowd in a booming voice. He raised a hand. "Back! Or you'll all be burned to death!"

The crowd retreated. Again Tristam moved with them, clutching the girl tightly around the waist and half-carrying her to keep her from falling under the scrambling feet. Several nearby tents had caught fire, and their smoke was rising in spiraling columns, thick and black. On their other side the roof of one of the permanent buildings was beginning to smoke, though no flames were yet visible there.

"We must push our way into one of the inns," Tristam told Callie. "That is our only hope. Hold tightly to my hand."

"But wait," she protested. "I am going to drop Lady Godiva, and some heartless ruffian will throw her into the flames."

Tristam quickly took the puppet and stuffed it into the front of his shirt. Then, clasping Callie's wrist in a powerful grip, he leaned into the milling crowd. Slowly he began to force his way toward the inn.

For a few seconds it appeared as though they were

finally going to make good their escape as they inched toward their goal. But suddenly the crowd surged back from a nearby wall, and again they were carried along with it. This time, however, to their relief, they were being shoved toward the open section of the fair. Tristam yielded quickly and began to feel a flicker of hope; but almost immediately there was another surge, and this time a huge red-faced yokel fell against his arm, and Callie's hand was torn away.

He planted his feet. Parting like a river that has been breached by an island, the crowd flowed past on either side of him. He could see Callie borne off by one relentless stream that swept in a curving path, back toward the fire. The blaze was now a raging inferno, throwing towering columns of furious red fire into the sky. To Tristam's horror he watched the river of humanity rush like a stream of lemmings toward its own destruction. But at the last moment the vanguard swerved around an unseen obstacle and flowed back toward him. Over the top of the crowd he could see that Callie had lost her bonnet; her shining blond head bobbed in a path around a blazing fruit stand, then back toward him. He readied himself to catch hold of her as she passed; but abruptly the flood changed direction again, and she was pushed toward the walls of the permanent buildings. To his dismay he saw that one of them—an inn—was now burning furiously. The crowd also made this discovery and surged to a halt, milling in a disorderly circle.

By this time the heat from the burning wall was so

intense that Tristam retreated a few steps. There was a jangle of shattering glass as a window exploded, then great blasts of flame spewed out, scattering sparks in a steady shower over the spectators. The crowd quickly drew together and retreated. With a resounding crash a wall to their left collapsed, spitting flames and cinders in all directions; and as soon as the clouds of smoke no longer obscured his view, Tristam saw that Callie had somehow been driven toward the burning inn, then abandoned. She now stood alone in a cul de sac which was formed by the rear walls of three permanent buildings, her retreat partially blocked by the furiously burning pile of rubble from the fallen wall. There was one small window set into the far wall, but it was far above her reach. Her only possible escape was through a narrow aperture which remained between the standing wall and the molten inferno, but there were such angry waves of heat rising from the burning debris that Tristam was sure her billowing skirt would ignite if she tried to run through the gap. On the other hand, if she remained where she was, she would be consumed by flames within the next few minutes.

As he stood watching her, his heart sinking, she slumped to the ground and buried her face against her knees in the protective folds of her skirt; and suddenly Tristam felt the same wrench of pain he had experienced the day he was told that his father was dead.

He straightened his shoulders and, taking a deep breath, plunged across the cobbles toward the edge of the inferno. He was aware of shouts from bystanders; a large man in a blackened apron rushed forward to intercept him, but he leaped past him and raced alongside the boiling flames, throwing up a hand to shield the side of his face. Even though he had steeled himself, expecting the raging air to sear his skin as he rushed past, he was unprepared for the intensity of the pain that struck him—as though thousands of razors were slicing his face. Inside the cul de sac the heat was undiminished. He dared not breathe.

Callie had crawled back against the farthest wall, and the face which she raised to him was red and dripping with perspiration. Without a word he grabbed her and jerked her to her feet; then, lifting her high over his head, he shoved her through the little window. She disappeared in a tumble of petticoats, one of her slippers dropping off and landing against his right ankle.

Then, and only then, did he face the fact that he was about to die—and painfully—for there was no longer a route back through the fire. The building on the other side of the collapsed wall had now begun to burn furiously, and any possible retreat was completely blocked by flames.

It was strange, he thought suddenly, that he had finally done something which would cause the members of the ton to turn to each other and say, "Indeed, Lord Ansel was fortunate to have had such a son"—but it was too late for him to derive any pleasure from it. In fact, he no longer cared.

By this time the roar of the flames drowned out every other sound. He cringed back against the farthest wall, under the window, struggling to draw some air into his lungs but reluctant to do so as he knew that the searing heat would burn them to a crisp. Crouching against the stones, he was steeling himself, preparing to take a deep breath and bring his life quickly to an end when he became aware of activity above him. He peered up at the window. A large piece of wood was coming out, suddenly popping through the aperture like a cork being ejected from the neck of a bottle, and a moment later Callie appeared, falling halfway out as she hung on to the rung of a huge Spanish chair and dropped it down the side of the building. Tristam leaped to his feet, catching the chair before it could fall onto the stones and splinter a leg. Immediately he set it against the wall, stepped up onto the seat, then onto the apex of its heavy carved back, caught hold of the window frame, and swung a leg over the sill. A moment later he had fallen into the room beyond and felt the life-giving rush of cooler air wash over him.

"My God!" he exclaimed, inhaling deeply. "What a remarkable girl you are to have your wits about you at a time like this."

"Please!" she begged, trying to pull him to his feet. "We must find our way out of this building. The flames are already roaring in the attics."

Catching hold of one of his hands, she pulled him onto his knees and began dragging him toward the doorway. He staggered to his feet and scrambled after her. Beyond the low opening they found a hall-way, then a narrow staircase which led down into a flagged entryway. Showers of sparks were already falling around them. Throwing open the front door, they hurled themselves out into the street, barely avoiding a rush of flames that engulfed the building and spewed out of every opening. They plunged across the street to an open cobbled square.

On one side the owners of the burning buildings had recruited a fire line, which was passing buckets of water to a pair of stalwarts at their head. These worthies were slinging the water onto the blazing edifices, though with a notable lack of effect. As Tristam and Callie stumbled out, a plume of flame licking at their heels, the firemen retreated in disorder and milled distractedly in the center of the square.

But after a tirade of spectacular curses from one of the owners a degree of order was restored and the fire brigade reformed, turning its attention to several buildings beyond the blaze which had not as yet burst into flame. Someone found a ladder and went trotting back and forth with it, scattering spectators and workers as he swung it around their heads. The men who had comprised the original fire line again began to pass buckets along its length.

Tristam drew Callie to one side, beyond the turmoil, and procured a reed chair from a kindly merchant. She sank onto it, letting out an enormous sigh of relief.

"It is hard to realize that we have escaped with no more damage than the loss of a shoe," she said. "Please accept my gratitude, sir; I owe my life to your heroism."

"Indeed not!" he told her. "It is I who am indebted to you!"

"No, no! I did nothing extraordinary."

"But you did," he insisted. "At great personal risk you delivered the means for my escape."

"But it was you who rushed so unselfishly into the flames."

They had both set their jaws in preparation for a lengthy debate when they were interrupted by a shout, and pushing his way through the crowd, Brandy appeared with Rowan panting at his heels.

"Thank God we've found you alive!" he cried. "We saw you at the top of the Ups and Downs and feared you were victims of this horrifying affair."

"We most certainly should have been," Callie told him, "if Lord Tristam had not displayed the most wonderful courage."

"No, no," he insisted. "Her heroism was at least as remarkable as mine."

"Well, at any rate," Brandy said, "I thank you profoundly for keeping my sister safe."

Tristam had a faraway look in his eye. "It is strange," he mused. "I have discovered that every person becomes a hero when the circumstances demand it."

"Not every person, certainly," Brandy objected.

"Almost every person," Tristam said.

"Nonsense!" Rowan said. "I have never committed an heroic act in my life and never shall. Very few persons are heroes or heroines. We must acknowledge the fact that Tris and Miss Belcroft"—he bowed elaborately toward Callie—"are exceptional individuals, of great valor, and we must let it be known to all the ton that they have comported themselves in this most remarkable way."

Callie and Tristam both raised their hands in protest.

"Please, no accolades," Tristam urged him. "I would find them most discomfiting."

"And I," Callie agreed.

"Ah, well," Brandy said, sliding an arm around his sister's shoulder, "the important thing is that you are both safe and . . ." He paused, staring at the front of Tristam's soot-ravaged waistcoat. "What is that sinister bulge in the front of your shirt, old man?"

Tristam looked down at his own middle, then with a wry smile pulled the puppet out into view.

"Good God!" Brandy laughed. "It's Lady Godiva, and she's naked as an onion! Get rid of her before we're dragged off for lewd conduct. Throw her onto the fire!"

"No, no!" Callie cried, taking the doll from Tristam's hands and cradling it in her arms. "Such a spirited little creature! We shall return her to her rightful owner."

"I fear he no longer has any use for her," Brandy told her. "His tent has burned and he has run off."

"Then I shall keep her safe until he needs her again."

Brandy chuckled. Pulling a large linen handkerchief out of his pocket, he carefully wrapped it around the lady's body and secured it under her chin. "Now you may feel easy about appearing in her company," he told his sister. "And let us all go off in search of our carriage. There is nothing we can do

150

here, and this area is becoming more dangerous every minute, I fear."

"Yes, I have lost a slipper and must hobble about in a state of semidishabille," Callie pointed out. "The sooner I am tucked discreetly out of sight, the better."

"Ah," Rowan murmured, "a warm bath and a proper lunch will have us all feeling more the thing in no time, I have no doubt."

Chapter 13

When Tristam arrived at his town house, purring happily to himself despite the rigors of his day at Bartholomew Fair, he was astonished to find that his mother had arrived from Marcourt and was pacing distractedly back and forth in the library, wringing her hands. At sight of him she let out a squeak and rushed into his arms.

"Oh, Tristam, my dearest!" she cried. "They said you had gone to Bartholomew Fair, and we have been watching columns of hideous smoke rising from that quarter. We are told that the flames are moving this way and that all London will be burned to the ground before the conflagration is brought under control."

"Nonsense," her son said, patting her hand gently. "The fire was subsiding when I came away."

"Well, thank heaven for that!" she said. "I am delighted to know that London will be spared. But I have had the most dreadful, frightening letter from Seffronia, and I felt that I must come to you immediately and reveal its awful contents."

"Indeed?" he said in a quelling tone. "I trust she has not said anything derogatory about her niece."

"Well, my dearest, I fear that she has. I had come to the conclusion that it was necessary for us to arrive at the truth, so I wrote and asked her to reveal the details of her niece's affliction—in the most tactful possible manner, of course. And the letter I received in return . . ." She clasped her hands together and let out a tragic sigh. "Of course, I could not bring myself to read it, suspecting what dreadful sorrows were contained therein. But dear Amanda Blankenthorpe was with me—most fortuitously—and it would have wrung your heart to hear her read those heartrending words aloud to me."

Tristam, listening impatiently, began to bite at his lower lip. "Do you, by any chance, have the letter with you, Mama?"

"Yes, I do."

She dove into her reticule and drew out a rumpled piece of paper which bore the evidence of much handling and the marks of many tears, which had splattered across the main body of the missive.

"You can see how the pathos of it affected poor, dear Amanda," she said, pointing with a finger to one of the smudges. "She wept most piteously at these dreadful revelations."

Tristam, whose eyes were rapidly scanning the page, scowled. "What revelations could she have found so moving, I wonder? I find it difficult to make any sense at all out of this rhetoric. Listen to this, for example: 'Of course it has always been my dearest hope—but you are aware of my sentiments on that

153

head.' And here she says, 'Why is the world so cruel, my dearest Gracia, when the simplest pleasures would give us the greatest joy? Why are we denied the warm relationships which would turn emptiness to fulfillment?' What the devil can she mean by that?"

"It is obvious, my dearest," Lady Gracia explained, "that she is referring to her unhappy niece. She means that the world is cruel in rendering her mad, and that if it were not so, she herself would be able to enjoy a warm relationship with the girl."

"But the facts of the matter are that she does enjoy a warm relationship with the girl," Tristam told her. "I have seen them together, and their affection is boundless." He peered down at the letter again. "In fact, there is not one reference to her niece's affliction in this entire communication. Callie's name does not even appear. Indeed, it is probable that she refers to the cruelty of your separation from each other since you have become a recluse at Marcourt or to the cruelty of my father's untimely demise."

"But I wrote to her requesting information about her niece," Lady Gracia pointed out. "Why should she answer me by discussing your father?"

Tristam nodded. "That is strange, of course. What precisely did you say to her in your letter? Did you ask her pointblank whether Callie is mad?"

Lady Gracia threw up her hands. "How can you suggest such a thing? Certainly I could not be so crude. I invited her in the most delicate possible way to confide in me."

"I see," Tristam said, scanning the first few lines

again. "And she has expressed her devotion to you here. 'Of course, my dearest friend, my deepest gratitude goes out to you for your generous affection for me, and I shall lean on your rock forever.' What rock, pray, is she referring to?"

"Our friendship, like a rock everlasting—that sort of thing."

"Yes. And then she goes on to commiserate with you over the loss of my father . . ."

"No, no, my dearest," she protested, taking the letter gently from his hand. "She bemoans the condition of her beloved niece."

Tristam shook his head firmly. "She distinctly says here, 'your loss.' That must refer to my father."

"I had thought she meant . . ." Lady Gracia began. Then she paused to frown at the paper, running her finger along one of the lines. "Well, perhaps I am mistaken."

"I fear so," Tristam agreed. "What has happened is that you have written her a tactful letter which has said nothing; and she has written you an equally obscure reply. I think there is nothing for it but to ask her, 'What is the truth about your niece?'—if you expect to receive the answer, that is."

"We cannot do that, my love! If she does not wish to confide in us, there is no way we can intrude upon her secret agonies."

"And I have no intention of doing so," her son told her. "I am convinced that all these malicious rumors are nonsense. Considering the splendid manner in which Callie conducted herself this morning at the fair, despite the horrendous ordeal to which we

155

were subjected, I am confident that her reason is as sound as yours or mine. In fact, if she had not been quick-witted and in complete control of her faculties, I should not be standing here before you at this moment. In short, she saved my life."

"She what? Impossible!"

"But a fact. And feeling as I do about the girl, I am going to put aside all my reservations and offer for her."

"Offer for her!" Gracia cried, taking three wobbly steps to the right and two toward the left, all the while wringing her hands. "You don't even know her, my darling. You must find another girl who will captivate you. Have you considered Ariadne Devonwell? Such an exquisite, Junoesque young lady and so pretty behaved."

Turning toward a window, Tristam pushed the curtain aside with a hand and stared unhappily out into the square. "There is no doubt in your mind, is there, Mama, that the truth about Callie Belcroft will be thoroughly shattering, when all is revealed to us?"

She shook her head. "There have been so many dreadful stories about the girl . . . and where there is smoke, there is fire, you know."

Tristam scowled. "If indeed it is smoke. Perhaps instead it is only fog or steam, or some other vapor. I wonder how many innocents have been damned by that abominable phrase, 'Where there's smoke, there's fire.' "

With a sigh he stood watching a curricle trot into view outside the window and draw up in front of the house next door. The Earl of Eggford, resplendent as usual in the latest kick of fashion and without so much as a hair displaced by his recent drive, tossed his reins negligently to his tiger and stepped onto the curb.

Now there, Tristam thought to himself, *is a man of note! I could wish he would get wind of my adventures at Bartholomew Fair . . .*

But as Eggford was handing his whip to a groom, around a nearby corner danced Morgan Fenn, taking four steps forward, then rocking backward one step, then jigging vigorously through eight clog steps before progressing forward again in the same pattern. Catching sight of Eggford, he capered over to him, sweeping off his hat in greeting and performing an extra measure of pas for his benefit.

"What are you watching, my dearest?" Gracia asked her son.

Tristam chuckled. "It's Morgan doing a little dance for his friend, Eggford. They're great chums, are they not? I seem to remember them visiting Marcourt together years ago when they were both at Oxford."

"Indeed, yes," Gracia agreed. "Had digs together, as they say, and were inseparable." She laughed softly to herself. "What a charming boy Morgan was, was he not?"

"Good God!" Tristam exclaimed as he watched Eggford stiffen and turn haughtily away from Fenn, "he's cutting Morg! Is that possible?"

Gracia sighed. "So sad that Morgan has become such a—what would you children call him, a loose screw?—a mortification for the entire family."

Tristam snorted. "I shall run outside and greet him affectionately before Eggford is out of earshot."

Before he could move away from the window, another carriage rattled into view—this time a high perch phaeton with none other than the Prince Regent himself at the ribbons. At sight of Fenn he smiled and greeted him with a regal but cordial gesture. Eggford, who was halfway to his own front door, abandoned his dignity and scrambled back down his walkway, sweeping off his hat and bowing elaborately to the Regent. Prinny was past him, however, and disappeared around the corner, without a backward glance. Eggford straightened himself. For a moment he stood glaring into the distance; then, striking a more imperious pose than ever, he looked pointedly through his ex-friend, turned his back on him, and proceeded stiffly up his front walk.

"My dearest," Gracia reminded her son, "you were about to invite your cousin inside."

"Yes," he agreed, rubbing his chin thoughtfully. "Do you know, Mama, I believe I have learned the most valuable lesson of my entire life today."

"Indeed? What is that, pray?"

He hesitated. "I must sort it all out, of course, but it has to do with one's attitude toward oneself—and the approval of Society."

"Yes, yes," she exclaimed, "the admiration of Society is of prime importance."

"No, it is not," he said quickly. "It is all dross. What is of prime importance is one's opinion of oneself."

Lady Gracia looked at him blankly. "Is that true,

my love? I am not quite sure what you mean. But I do know that the right thing to do at this moment is to invite Morgan into the house for a cup of tea and a bit of cake; and if you do not do so at once, he will have passed by us, and we shall have been lax in our duty."

"That is true," Tristam agreed, and strode quickly to the front door.

Eggford was still in sight when he reached the front steps. To his surprise he discovered Fenn almost at his feet, striding up the front walk, humming to himself and gracefully executing the figures of a country dance—three jogs forward, two back, then a piaffer, trotting vigorously in place, finishing with a little cabriole to the right and one to the left before he began again and repeated the measure.

Tristam glanced toward the house next door and saw that Eggford was scurrying toward his entry-way. "Morgan, old man!" Tristam called in a huge voice. "How kind of you to grant us your company! Come in, come in! My mother will be delighted to see you."

Fenn was singing stridently through his nose, "Tum tum ta tum tiddy tum tum." He executed a final leap, a pirouette, and swept off his hat in an elaborate bow.

"Ah, Tris," he breathed, pausing to exhale and inhale heavily, "what a *glorious* day! You see before ye a new an' better man!"

"I do?" Tristam said, momentarily thrown off stride. As far as he could ascertain, he was facing the same old Morgan—face flushed, eyes rheumy, clothing askew, with a heavy aroma of fermenting molasses forming a nimbus around him.

"You do, indeed!" Fenn assured him. "You have before ye a man who's been reformed by love." His face crumpled suddenly, and running the back of a sleeve across his eyes, he broke into a wild little dance, bounding and kicking in a circle until he had brought his emotions to heel.

Tristam caught him quickly by the elbow and hurried him in through the front door. "Come tell my mother," he said.

The marchioness was gliding across the vestibule toward them, her hands outstretched. "Morgan, my love," she crooned, "what a delightful surprise."

Fenn bowed elaborately. "Ah, dear lady, I have come to receive your blessing." His face twisted again. "I've been rescued from the quagmires of debauchery an' am settin' forth on a new path in life." Whipping out a handkerchief, he blew a clarion blast into it.

"But my dear boy," Gracia protested, "I cannot believe that you have ever been truly wicked."

"No, no," Tristam agreed. "You've been a scamp, Morg, but never a villain."

Fenn shook his head miserably. "I must confess to you, my nearest and dearest, I've been sucked down into the maelstrom o' depravity, lo these many years. Thank God I'm now to be saved!"

"Well, I'm delighted, I assure you," Lady Gracia told him. "How is this to be accomplished?"

Fenn inhaled jerkily. "Me darlin' Gwendolyn,

bless her heart; the dearest, the sweetest, the purest . . ."

His voice broke. Putting his handkerchief to his nose, he blew another tantara and cleared his throat. Then he tried to speak, but his voice cracked badly; and after a few ineffectual squawks he gave in to emotion and bowed over his handkerchief, allowing the tears to flow freely down his cheeks.

"Here, here, now," Tristam chided, thumping him reassuringly on the back. "You must buck up, old man. Don't go to pieces in front of your aunt. You know how sympathetic she is."

"Yes," Lady Gracia agreed, pulling a tiny lace handkerchief out of her sleeve and dobbing at the tears which were already beginning to well up in her eyes. "You must not cry, my love. I cannot bear to see my dear ones suffer."

"But I'm not sufferin', Aunty," he bubbled. "I'm so filled wi' joy, it's runnin' over!" He slid an arm around her waist and kissed her lightly on the cheek; then, attacked by a fresh tide of sensibility, he blubbered unrestrainedly onto the marchioness's neck. She let out a sob.

"Good God!" Tristam muttered. "Mama, you must stop immediately." She was breathing jerkily and dobbing at her eyes. "Morg!" he scolded. "You must brace up for my mother's sake."

But his chiding and pleading were to no avail. Fenn continued to weep with abandon while Lady Gracia leaned against him and joined a soprano obbligato to his dirge. Finally Tristam was obliged to call for strong spirits and ply both sufferers with brandy. They immediately showed promise of recovery, but it was not until he had managed to usher them to separate sofas and seat them some distance apart that he was able to distract them and restore a modicum of tranquility to the scene.

"Now let us delve into the history of this remarkable girl," Tristam urged. "Who is she, Morg?"

"The steady hand this wayward b'y requires," Fenn told him in a feeble voice.

"Yes, yes, but *who?*"

Lady Gracia was busily waving her vinaigrette under her own nose. "Is she perhaps little Gwendolyn Welles? I remember her so fondly from the time she was a child; delightful little creature with dimples and black ringlets."

"No," Fenn said quickly. "None of old Welles brood. That Gwendolyn married 'Booby' Chappell last year; and the month after, she ran off to the Continent with young Tremayne."

"Good gracious, how dreadful!" Gracia exclaimed. "Why did I not hear of it?"

Tristam laid a gentle hand on his mother's shoulder. "You were out of touch with the world, Mama, mourning my father."

"Ah, true," she agreed, stanching a fresh stream of tears.

"But *my* Gwendolyn," Fenn went on, "is a different sort, I assure you—faithful to the death."

"An heiress?" Tristam suggested.

"No, I fear not," he admitted. He hesitated a moment as he saw both his relatives begin to frown. "But she has so many treasures, my dears, to compensate for lack o' blunt. She's level-headed, I can tell you that, an' smart as a whip, an' "—he smiled impishly—"she's a stylish little creature."

Immediately his lips trembled, and he was obliged to put his handkerchief to his nose.

Lady Gracia raised her eyebrows. "Oh, she is pretty, then?"

"Not pretty, precisely," he told her, "but pleasin' to the eye."

Lady Gracia mused for a moment, her brow rumpled in a slight frown. "I wonder if you should not consider a bit longer before you commit yourself to this girl, my love. If she is not rich, she should at least be pretty."

"But, Mama," Tristam intervened, "in Morgan's case I feel that level-headedness in a wife is a sterling quality."

"True," she agreed, "as do I. Nevertheless, I feel that she should also be either pretty or rich."

There was a moment of silence before Fenn suggested, "Perhaps when you see her, Aunty, you'll find her pretty."

Lady Gracia brightened. "Will I indeed? Then she is comely, my dear?"

"If you was to put a ball gown on her and comb ringlets into her hair, I wager she'd charm the birds right out of the trees."

"Ah," Gracia said with a smile, "that is all right then."

Fenn's chin was beginning to quiver again. "But most important, Aunty, you see, I love her." He stopped to blow into his handkerchief. "She'll be the island in me sea o' troubles—the anchor for me ship o' life. She'll gie me the steadiness I require to obtain a bountiful annuity. Then I'll have me a brood o' bouncin' bairns climbin' about me knees an' pressin' their soft little cheeks against mine."

Lady Gracia wiped her eyes. "You must bring this charming girl to see me, my love. I shall meet her and give you my opinion."

Fenn pulled out his pocket watch and studied it. "I knew you'd be gracious and kindly, as always, Aunty. If me timepiece is correct, she'll arrive in three minutes."

"Oh, indeed?" Gracia exclaimed. "Then we must order a special tea." She waved a hand at her son. "Please alert Murdoch to our needs, my love." She turned back to her nephew. "Now you must tell me all I need to know about her, dear. What are her antecedents?"

"Well"—he hesitated—"I'll not be able to tell you that, ma'am, as I know nothing of them."

"Is that possible?" Gracia exclaimed. "Certainly the young lady's family name can tell us something."

"That's the thing, you see; she says her name is Smith—which I rather doubt—and there is nowhere to go from there."

"My dear," Lady Gracia said, leaning across a considerable distance to place a gentle hand on her nephew's arm, "you must consider this match more seriously. You must not be hasty. If you know nothing at all of the young lady . . ."

"I know everything that matters!" he cried. "I know she's trim an' dainty an' quiet an' proper, an'

164

she'll brook no nonsense from the likes o' me—makes me quieten down an' behave myself when I'm carried away by a fit o' mischief. There's no doubt in me mind that she'll . . ."

He was interrupted by the clatter of the front-door knocker. The three occupants of the drawing room exchanged speaking glances as Murdoch's feet clicked rhythmically across the vestibule floor. Then there was the sound of muffled voices in the lobby, and Murdoch appeared in the doorway. He inclined his head stiffly, his face an expressionless mask.

"With your permission, your ladyship, there is a young person who is requesting to see you. I have seated her in the hall."

"Oh, dear!" Gracia exclaimed, leaping to her feet. "Can it be Miss Smith? You should have brought her in to us immediately." Before Murdoch could justify his actions, she rushed out of the room. Fenn and Tristam scrambled after her.

Tristam's first sight of Gwendolyn revealed approximately what he had expected: a small, conservatively dressed young woman in a dark-green merino walking dress and a matching bonnet with only one green ostrich plume curling around her face. Her hair was arranged so simply as to appear austere, and she was sitting with her eyes demurely downcast and the tips of her black kid boots barely showing beneath her skirt.

"Gwendolyn, my love!" Fenn bellowed.

The girl rose smoothly to her feet and performed a dignified curtsy toward the marchioness.

"My dear child," Lady Gracia exclaimed, "how good of you to visit me."

"Thank you, madam," the girl responded in a low and remarkably steady voice. "How kind of you to receive me."

"You must tell me all about yourself," Gracia urged. She caught Gwendolyn's hand and, slipping it through her own arm, guided her toward the drawing room door. For a moment Tristam thought the girl was going to hold back; but then she allowed herself to be led forward, although there was a marked rigidity apparent in her posture.

Lady Gracia seated herself on a little satin sofa and pulled Gwendolyn down beside her. "Now, my dear," she said, "I would like to know where you were reared."

"In Sussex, ma'am," Gwendolyn told her, keeping her gaze fixed on her small gloved hands. "But London is now my home."

"Your family still lives in the country, I trust."

"No, ma'am."

Fenn brushed away a tear. "She's an orphan, poor lassie."

"Oh," Gracia said, her chin trembling. "Poor child."

Tristam, clearing his throat, quickly stepped forward. "Miss, er, Smith, what my mother is asking you is who your people are. Is it possible that you are somehow related to the Smith-Montagues who have been at Scunning Grange for so many centuries?"

"No, sir," Gwendolyn said, shaking her head gently. "I am not related to anyone of importance. I am

166

merely Miss Smith, now of London, with no connections of any sort."

Lady Gracia was heard to inhale unevenly.

"But," Tristam insisted, "you must be related to someone."

"No, sir, I am not."

"My dear Gwendolyn," Fenn began.

She raised a hand. "Please, Mr. Fenn, do not persist in addressing me as Gwendolyn. I have told you repeatedly that Lady Dolwyn has named me Mary."

Lady Gracia raised her head. "Lady Dolwyn? You are related to dear Arabella, then?"

"No, ma'am," Gwendolyn said. "I am one of Lady Dolwyn's nursemaids."

The marchioness's mouth fell open.

"One of her nursemaids?" Tristam said, looking at the girl. As he examined her more closely, he realized that she was the nursemaid with whom he had seen his cousin dancing around the square in front of Belcroft House the day before.

"Did Mr. Fenn not explain this?" she began. Abruptly she rose to her feet. "No, I perceive that he did not."

"Please, my dear," Lady Gracia urged in a faint voice, "you must give us some time to grow accustomed to this match. No one in our family has ever married a nursemaid before."

"Married!" the girl exclaimed. She turned to Tristam and, raising her eyes to his for the first time, gave him a piercing look. He was startled to see that she had a sharp little face with bright, small animal eyes, like a ferret's. Immediately she turned her gaze away and resumed the appearance of a prim young servant.

"Morgan," Tristam said quickly, turning to his cousin, "is this not the young lady you met in the park yesterday when you and I parted?"

Fenn nodded miserably.

"You knew her previously, of course?"

"No, sir," the girl said quickly. "We met only yesterday."

"But I knew at once she was the girl o' my dreams," Fenn blubbered. "I knew it was a match made in heaven."

Gwendolyn bowed stiffly. "With your permission, ma'am," she said to the marchioness, "I shall take myself off. Mr. Fenn made no mention of marriage when he invited me here, and he did not specify that your ladyship was a peeress—only some relation he wished me to meet. Please excuse my presumption." She walked quickly toward the door.

"Darlin'!" Fenn cried, leaping to his feet and scampering after her. "My love!" But the girl walked briskly out of the room without looking back at him. "Excuse me, Aunty," he called from the door. "Tris . . ." He disappeared into the vestibule. A moment later, as Lady Gracia and Tristam sat staring at each other in bewilderment, they heard the front door close sharply.

"Well!" Lady Gracia said. "How can that brazen creature have contrived such a hold over that poor, innocent boy? Somehow we must stop this match, for my dear mama always maintained most stoutly that no member of the upper classes could ever be happy married to a servant—though precisely why that should be so, I am sure I cannot tell you."

"I must confess that I don't see why it should be the case," Tristam observed, rising and wandering to the window. "Morgan is in dire need of a steadying influence, and whom do we know in his own class who would undertake such a task?"

Gracia sighed. "No one, I am sure. Whatever is to be done?"

She was silent for a moment, apparently deep in thought; then she announced, "You must take him under your wing, my love. You must invite him to Marcourt and show him the right way to go. And we shall introduce him to a delightful, strong-minded heiress who will know what to do with him. Perhaps Ariadne Devonwell; she is a most excellent and upright young lady."

"Mama!" Tristam protested. "Endeavoring to reform Morg is a fruitless task, as you well know. We have all attempted it and failed. And no young lady —excellent and upright, as you say—will saddle herself with such a nodcock."

"We need not tell dear Ariadne that he is susceptible to demon rum," Gracia went on without heeding him. "We can tell her that he has always been a high-strung child, that he has . . ." She rubbed her brow with her fingertips as she searched for a word.

"Has what?" Tristam prompted her. "Has fits, perhaps?"

"Good heavens, no!" her ladyship exclaimed. "Nothing so frightening. We shall tell her that he has periods of excitation, that he merely requires a firm, guiding hand—someone to give him the steadiness he occasionally lacks."

Tristam was gazing out the front window. At the foot of the steps Gwendolyn was standing with her hands planted firmly on her hips, advancing steadily on Fenn, her jaw wagging. He was retreating, shrugging his shoulders, raising his hands, and effecting various signs of acquiescence. Finally he was obliged to stop with his back against a wrought-iron paling while the girl raised a hand and wagged a finger furiously in his face.

"Good God!" Tristam exclaimed. "Mama, come look at this."

Lady Gracia scampered to his side in time to see Gwendolyn turn on her heel and stalk out the gate. Fenn scurried after her. He raised his arms in supplication. She continued her grim march. He broke into an Irish jig, dancing around her, waving his hat in her face, and leaping playfully. She strode relentlessly on.

As they neared the corner, Gwendolyn turned on Fenn suddenly and trod firmly on his toes, pinning one of his feet to the ground. Fenn floundered, waving both arms frantically. Before he could regain his balance, the girl raised a small fist and punched him hard on the nose. Then, releasing his foot, she marched off, her back turned with finality in his direction.

Fenn stood crumpled forward, one hand feeling gingerly for his nose. He examined his gloves, then drew out his handkerchief and applied it to the injured member. Pulling off his hat with his free hand, he ran the back of his sleeve across his brow. Then, squaring his shoulders, he bobbed off in pursuit of his beloved, waving one arm in a supplicating gesture, breaking into a jig for a few steps, then abandoning these tactics to trot after her, his jaw wagging steadily. The pair disappeared behind some shrubbery, Gwendolyn still marching with shoulders squared, and Fenn bowing and capering around her like a courting grouse.

"Dear, dear," Gracia said with a sigh. "One scarcely knows what to hope for. The boy is obviously in love with Gwendolyn. I wonder if perhaps she might be one of the Smith-Montagues after all and is concealing her connection because some dreadful tragedy has caused her branch of the family to fall upon hard times. Though I feel that, if it were the case, she might have been more communicative. Although, perhaps it is true, and she has turned her back forever on the upper classes."

"Why should she do that?" Tristam wondered.

"Bitterness?"

He shook his head. "Mama, you must not fabricate these explanations and spin elaborate stories when you have no facts at hand. You are only deceiving yourself."

She sighed. "It would be so much simpler if dear Gwendolyn were not a nursemaid."

"It would, indeed! But we must accept the fact that she is."

Lady Gracia walked slowly back to the sofa and seated herself. "There is nothing for it but that we must woo dear Morgan's affections away from her and focus them on someone who is more the thing. I shall apply myself to making a match between him and Ariadne Devonwell."

At that moment there were sounds in the vestibule and Morgan's voice rang out, "No, no, Murdoch, I shall announce myself." He clattered into the drawing room. "Aunty! Tristam!" He greeted them with a twisted grin. "Who'd have thought she'd be so set against marryin' above her station? You see before you a broken man!" He whipped out his handkerchief.

"Oh, my dear," Gracia sniffed, pulling out her own.

"No, no!" Tristam commanded. "Stop, both of you! Nothing will be accomplished by this nonsensical grief. We must apply ourselves to intelligently solving our problems."

"We have only one problem, old man," Fenn sniffed. He paused a moment to rub at his nose. "Well, two, actually: Gwendolyn's rejected me once an' for all; an' I've received a dun from Weston, which had completely slipped my mind."

"Don't worry about Weston," Tristam told him. "I'll pay him and take it out of your next quarter's check."

"But that's the thing, don't you see?" Fenn explained. "The bill's for three hundred pounds; and if you take it out of my next quarter, I'll not have enough to live on."

"You'll have three hundred and twenty-five pounds."

"Which is nothing," Fenn pointed out. "Just think

how you'd feel if you was obliged to live on a hundred quid per month."

Tristam smiled. "I rarely spend more than that, Morg."

"What!" his cousin exclaimed. "I'd be surprised if you spent as little as that every day, with your estates and farms and mills and all."

"But those don't count," Tristam told him. "I'm speaking of personal expenses; and I think I've come to realize the only solution to your problem. Why don't you just go ahead and reform yourself without relying on a wife? You can do it; and then you'll obtain that bountiful annuity you were speaking of." He nodded with satisfaction. "The annuity sounds like an excellent thing. Where's it to come from?"

"From you, of course."

"From me!" Tristam cried.

"Of course, lad. There's no doubt in me mind that when I prove meself worthy, you'll cough up the blunt to feed me bairns an' me sweet little wifie—not to mention providin' a proper home for 'em."

Tristam ran a hand over his brow. "And what sort of 'proper home' do you have in mind? Carlton House or the Brighton Pavilion?"

Fenn scowled at him. "For shame, laddie, mockin' me. I'd not expect anythin' grand. Somethin' more on the order o' that nice little pile on your Bellmer estate."

Tristam started. "You mean Collingrood? I've given the Pembertons a twenty-year lease on it. You know that."

"Indeed? That's a shame, to be sure. Then I'd not

say nay t' the little old Queen Anne house on the lower Troville meadows."

"Aunt Clara is there."

"She'll not last forever, poor darlin'. An' she'd be glad to have me livin' with 'er; always liked me, did Aunt Clara."

Tristam leaned back against the edge of a heavy table and pondered. "Tell you what I'll do, Morg. If you can steady yourself and stay on the straight and narrow for six months, I'll give you a lease on the Queen Anne house. You'll have to take care of Aunt Clara—that'll be part of it—and I'll give you only a one-year lease, to be renewed each January. But it's yours if you wish to make the effort."

"Grand, grand, grand!" Fenn cried, breaking into a jig and capering joyously around a sofa. He rounded the end and executed a complicated step in front of his aunt, catching her arm and swinging her in a circle. She squealed.

"Yes, yes," Tristam told him. "Enough of this nonsense, now. How do you intend to go about turning yourself into a paragon?"

Fenn released Lady Gracia and stood rubbing his chin thoughtfully. "Well, first I shall renounce John Barleycorn; I can see no way around that."

Tristam nodded. "Excellent beginning. And then?"

Fenn made a sweeping gesture with an arm. "I shall tot up m' debts and write out a schedule for payin' them off one by one. An' I shall renounce all unsteady companions an' form a new coterie o' friends."

"Yes, yes," Lady Gracia agreed. "That is excellent. And I suggest that you might attend church services every morning. It will reform your character in no time. There are so many excellent lessons that are read from the pulpit every day. Only this morning the Reverend Mr. Johnson was reading to us from Corinthians. No, that's wrong; I believe it was Acts. Well, whatever it was, it described the way Naomi followed Ruth into . . . was it Moab? Or was it Ruth who followed Naomi? Not that it makes any difference . . ."

Fenn had paled. "I don't feel I'd profit from sittin' in front of a spoutin' pulpit every mornin', Aunty. I can't feel that church is essential to the reform o' me character."

"I believe it might help a great deal, Morg," Tristam told him. "There's nothing like church to sober a man."

Fenn sighed heavily. "Very well. I'll attend church services every day. Please, Tris, if you'd pour a bit o' that brandy into a glass. I feel in need of a wee mite o' courage."

"Brandy!" his relatives both cried in unison.

"Oh, Morgan, my love, for shame!" Lady Gracia chided. "Not two minutes past you declared your determination to renounce strong spirits."

"And I shall! I shall!" Fenn assured her. "I shall start tomorrow."

Tristam shook his head. "You'll never start, Morg; admit it."

"I shall start!" Fenn cried. "I'll become the soberest man in England. I'll husband me blunt, an' never go into debt, an' live quiet an' proper as a country squire with me charmin' old aunty an' excellent wife. An' I'll start tomorrow first thing in the mornin'. Please pour a bit o' brandy into the glass."

With a sigh Tristam tipped a splash of cognac into a snifter and passed it to him.

"I'll straighten meself out," Fenn insisted, taking the glass into his hand and inhaling the fumes. "You'll see."

Lady Gracia was watching him thoughtfully, a crease between her brows. "Perhaps, my love, if you had a lovely young fiancee—like Gwendolyn, but a member of your own class—perhaps then you would have a stronger motive for following through with your reform."

"I've no doubt that's true," he agreed.

She took a deep breath. "Then I must introduce you to the most charming girl. Her name is Ariadne Devonwell, and she's an heiress."

"An heiress?" he said, brightening. "Not that I'm a mercenary man, you understand; but I wonder how much she would have."

"Twenty thousand."

"Indeed?" He passed the snifter back to Tristam. "I think I should like to meet this charming lady. Splash a bit more brandy there, Tris. As soon as I've refreshed myself, I'll be on my way an' get about the business of reformin' me character."

The following morning, when Tristam was ushered into the yellow saloon at Belcroft House, he found all three of his friends gathered there. Dressed in riding clothes, Brandy was hovering over the back of a sofa where Callie, radiant in an ivory muslin gown, was chatting affably with Rowan Dillworth. She was bending her head close to his while he held one of her hands and examined the palm.

"Dash it all, ma'am," Tristam heard him exclaim as he entered the room, "I see the most confusing sort of future here." He hesitated. "What is this line, I wonder? I've never seen a hand precisely like yours."

Brandy laughed. "I think you're quizzing us, Ro. Don't know the first thing about reading palms, I'll swear. Just an excuse for holding a young lady's hand—and a dashed clever one, at that."

Rowan began to protest, and Callie laughingly drew back; at that moment Brandy caught sight of Tristam in the doorway.

"Ah!" he called. "Here's a man to keep me company for a turn or two around the park. You rode, Tris?"

"I did," he said "But I had hoped to have a few words with Miss Belcroft."

"Sit down then," his friend said. "I'll wait until you've done the pretty."

Callie, looking over Rowan's shoulder at the new arrival, bestowed one of her devastating smiles on him, and Brandy, preparing to seat himself also, leaned a hand on the back of a nearby chair. But suddenly he scowled and drew back.

"Is this ugly old thing of Lord Davenant's still here? I should have thought that by this time our mother would have relegated it to an attic."

"She made three attempts to do so," Callie told him. "But our father was so angry—he insisted that the chair be returned to this room each time it was removed."

"I don't know what he is thinking of," Brandy snorted. "It should be tossed into the fire instead of left about to soil our hands and clothing."

"It is no longer dirty," Callie corrected him. "It has been thoroughly cleaned."

Tristam was considering the controversial chair. "It appears to be exceptionally sturdy—something which will even bear my weight safely. And I need not tell you that I often hesitate to settle my hulking frame on these delicate bits of twig and glue which are so capriciously dubbed 'chairs' and scattered about in London sitting rooms."

"Then seat yourself on it, by all means," Brandy urged, "and tell us whether the cabinetmakers of that other age knew how to construct a piece of furniture."

With a smile Tristam settled himself onto the chair. But to everyone s surprise, without the slightest hint of strain or sound of stress, the component parts of the chair began to disassemble under him. The legs separated from the seat, the arms fell away, the back quietly divided itself into three parts and collapsed. Callie, Rowan, and Brandy watched open-mouthed as Tristam dropped heavily to the floor. He landed with a horrendous crash, his head smacking sharply against the wall behind him. For a moment he looked at his companions in bewilderment; then he closed his eyes and passed from consciousness.

"Oh!" Callie wailed, rushing to his side and dropping onto her knees beside him.

"Wait!" Brandy warned. "Don't touch him! We must be certain we do not injure him further."

"Good God!" Rowan exclaimed. "Look at his arm, Brandy! Such a wretched break!"

"Yes, yes," Brandy said quickly. "I shall send someone for a surgeon immediately. Take that cushion there and put it under his head."

But Rowan, who had turned a greenish shade of gray, clapped a hand over his mouth and departed abruptly through a french window into the garden. The next moment a door on the opposite side of the room flew open and Regina leaped in, laughing gleefully.

"Ha, ha!" she shouted in triumph. But at the sight of Tristam's crumpled form she stopped in shocked surprise. "It's not Osgood," she said.

Brandy planted his fists on his hips. "Not Osgood! Indeed, is it possible *you* engineered this atrocity Mama?"

I never intended that Tristam should be involved. Nor anyone else but your odious father."

"However," he pointed out sternly, "you gave very little thought to where the ends of your mischief might carry us."

Regina was staring at Tristam's silent face, her chin quivering. With a stifled sob she disappeared into the hall.

"Oh, Brandy," Callie whispered, laying a hand gently against Tristam's ashen cheek, "we must get help immediately. I fear my mother has killed him."

"No, no," he assured her. "I can't believe Tristam is so fragile as that. But I'll wager he's going to feel dashed uncomfortable when he comes to."

At that moment Rimpson hurried into the room, stared at Tristam's ruined arm, and exclaimed, "Good heavens, sir!"

"Yes," Brandy agreed. "Send someone immediately to fetch Sir Neville, and be sure to explain to him that Lord Tristam's arm is broken. Then let us see if we can make him more comfortable until help arrives. I shall wish James and Collins and Foster in here to carry him to bed as soon as he rouses."

Rimpson scurried away to undertake his errands, and Brandy took a cushion from one of the sofas and knelt beside Tristam's head. He was gently trying to raise him when his friend opened his eyes.

"Brandy," he murmured. "What the devil?"

"It's all right," Brandy assured him. "Well, not all right, I must admit It's a dashed rotten shame! But Sir Neville will soon be here to put you back together.

"Put me back . . ." He turned his head slowly, winced, then caught sight of Callie's stricken face. Tears were pouring down her cheeks.

"Such terrible things have been happening to Lord Tristam these two days," she sniffled, "since he has been in my company. Yesterday he nearly perished in the flames; today his arm has been broken—perhaps his head. It's as though I'm a sort of evil charm." She turned miserably to her brother. "In addition to all the other horrors I must endure,

Brandy, is it possible that I am bad luck to everyone I care about?"

"Certainly not!" Brandy protested. "Such nonsense!"

"Horrors you must endure?" Tristam asked. "What do you mean?"

Brandy scowled. "Nothing. Nothing at all."

"But Brandy," she chided, "you must not say 'nothing.' You must not pretend that I am free of the staggering burden I bear."

"Nonsense!" he protested. "You are much better since you came to town. Admit it. You are much easier in your mind."

Before Callie could answer, Rimpson bustled in with three large men at his heels and a tray in his hands.

"Would you wish to give his lordship a bit of cognac, sir?"

"Yes, please," Tristam said, opening his eyes briefly "It would perhaps numb my arm somewhat —though how it will affect my headache is another matter."

"Good God, Tris, I'm sorry about this!" Brandy exclaimed, kneeling beside his friend and holding a glass to his lips. "How my mother could have perpetrated such a fiendish prank is beyond my ken."

Callie covered her face with her hands and began to weep softly again. "I feel certain I am somehow the cause of his suffering. I bring unhappiness to everything I touch. I shall enter a nunnery."

"Good God!" Brandy shrieked. "How can you speak of nunneries at a time like this! You're not to enter one, do you understand me? I forbid it! And I forbid you ever to mention nunneries again!"

Callie scrambled to her feet and fled toward the door; but Brandy, aware that his response had been unnecessarily savage, leaped up and rushed after her, throwing an arm firmly around her shoulders and dragging her to a halt.

"Here, here, now, popsy," he urged, "buck up. None of this is your fault, and you must not think it. The blame is entirely our parents'. But now, you see, we must try to make Tris feel easier—we must get him onto a comfortable couch and set his arm. So run along and leave us to our work. I'll send someone to you with word of our progress."

Tristam's eyes were now open, and as Callie cast a tearful glance in his direction, he gave her a feeble smile. With a choked sob she rushed out of the room.

Some twenty minutes later, as she was still endeavoring to compose herself in her bedroom, she heard a clattering in the hallway outside her door and, peeping out, discovered Brandy and his three stalwart assistants passing by with Tristam hanging precariously in their midst. The victim, catching sight of her tearstained face and having been fortified by a robust noggin of cognac, gave her a lopsided wink. The entourage had barely disappeared into a nearby guest room when Rimpson appeared, ushering Sir Neville and his two lieutenants, both of whom were heavily laden with bundles of surgical supplies. They also disappeared into the guest room.

As soon as the door had been firmly shut and a

degree of quiet again reigned in the upper stories of the house, Callie became aware of noises emanating from the public rooms below. There were roars and shrieks and sounds of stamping feet. She could hear her father shouting, "How dare you, madam! This marvelous chair is worth ten score of you! To wantonly destroy a priceless work of art . . ."

"If you do not wish it destroyed, remove it from this house!" Regina screamed. "I shall not have the hideous old relic set among our beautiful gilded chairs! We are the laughing stock of the ton!"

"This is *my* house!" Osgood shouted. "These are *my* chairs! I shall place them where I wish!"

"I shall take an ax to that filthy piece of rubbish if I find it in these public rooms again!"

"Madam, you should have your ears boxed!"

With a gasp Callie flew down the stairs toward the yellow saloon, from which the sounds of the quarrel were issuing. She had just reached the doorway when Regina stomped out, nearly colliding with her.

"Oh, my dear, be careful," her mother exclaimed, drawing to a halt. "Do not go into the yellow saloon. You must avoid that dreadful man at all costs. There is no telling what maniacal thing he will take it into his head to do next."

She stood for a moment with her own head high and eyes flaring. Suddenly she raised a finger to her lips. "Listen," she whispered.

Callie held her breath. "I don't see . . ." she began.

"Just as I thought!" Regina spat. "That odious . . . that monstrous . . . that *evil* man has left the door ajar into the blue saloon! There is no limit to his villainy!" Setting her lower jaw in a furious grimace, she marched back into the yellow drawing room. Callie scampered after her.

"Wait," she began, "please don't . . ." But Regina, ignoring her, stomped across the room, her arms pumping. The door into the blue saloon was indeed ajar, and Callie saw, to her bewilderment, that there was a pail balanced atop it.

"Mama!" she warned.

Regina, muttering darkly to herself, caught hold of the door and slammed it shut with a resounding crash. The pail, deprived of support, promptly flipped over and dumped its contents over her, then dropped onto her head, landing with a resounding clang. For a moment she stood motionless, the bucket drooping over her face and head. Then, with a watery gurgle of protest, she sank to the floor.

"Oh!" Callie cried, wringing her hands and rushing to her mother's side. "Help!"

Assistance, to her surprise, arrived in the form of Rowan Dillworth, who entered briskly from the garden, his face still gray.

"My dear Miss Belcroft!" he exclaimed, his eyes wide with bewilderment. "What sort of frolic is this, pray?"

To Callie's relief Brandy also strode into the room at that moment through the opposite door. "What's wrong with you, popsy? Why all the howls?"

Callie pointed to Regina.

"What the devil!" he cried, bending over the fallen combatant. "Mama, what in the name of heaven are you up to now?"

"It is not she," Callie explained. "Some vile prankster placed a pail of water . . ."

Before she could finish, the door opened and Lord Osgood leaned his head inside, grinning impishly. "Hee, hee, hee," he chortled. He found himself eye to eye with his irate son.

"Sir!" Brandy intoned, trembling with emotion. "Is it possible you are responsible for this? I cannot believe you capable of it!"

Rowan was kneeling beside Regina, tenderly lifting the bucket from her head. Raising her face to his, she peered at him through dazed eyes, her thoroughly wetted curls trailing down over her cheeks in dripping tendrils. Osgood, watching her out of the corner of his eye, giggled softly.

"Sir!" Brandy thundered. "Have you considered the consequences of these pranks? Upstairs Waivering lies suffering untold agonies from a broken arm; and it is only by the grace of God that you have not killed my mother."

Suddenly Osgood gave himself a shake. "Yes, yes," he said. "Of course you are right. This nonsense must end. It is apparent to me, if to no one else, that it is impossible for your mother and me to live under the same roof without dire consequences. I shall retire to Colter Abbey, and she shall remain here. Separated, perhaps we may both lead proper and productive lives. I shall immediately give orders to Rimpson, and he shall prepare for my journey home."

185

Chapter 14

After a sustaining lunch Lord Osgood departed for Colter Abbey in his curricle, his face wreathed in smiles. From her bedroom window Callie watched him wave cheerily to a friend who was passing by on foot. He paused a few moments to chat, then raised his whip in a debonair salute and clattered off down the street.

Thereafter, in deference to the invalids, a profound silence settled over Belcroft House. In the middle of the afternoon Lady Gracia made an appearance on Seffronia's arm, her face white and haggard, and visited her son's sickroom, where she found him heavily drugged and with his injured arm lying helplessly beside him, buttressed with cushions and covered by an enormous mound of white linen. She departed in even lower spirits than she had arrived.

A little after four o'clock, as Callie roused from a fitful nap, she became aware of new sounds in the hallway outside her room. Tiptoeing to the door, she gingerly put her head out. A gentleman in bottle-green trousers and a candy-striped waistcoat was leaning against the wall, his face buried in his arms and his shoulders shaking.

"Good heavens, sir," she cried, rushing to put a supportive hand under one of his elbows. "Are you ill?"

He raised a swollen face, and she saw that tears were coursing down his cheeks. "Not ill, dear lady; wrung by pity. I've been with me cousin, poor broken laddie."

"Please, sir," she urged, alarmed by his unhealthy color, "allow me to help you to a chair and offer you a bit of refreshment."

He brightened. "Ah, that would be the savin' o' me. You're a ministerin' angel. Thank ye, lass."

To her surprise, as she held him solicitously by the arm and led him down the hallway to the stairs, he appeared to grow progressively older and more infirm. He was obliged to lean heavily on the banister, and by the time they had reached the blue drawing room, he was limping visibly. It was only with the greatest difficulty that she was able to settle him onto a sofa, and by that time he appeared to be so frail that she feared he would collapse and roll off onto the floor the moment she released him. Instead, he sagged back against the cushions and, drawing a handkerchief from a pocket, pressed it to his nose and blew into it with startling vigor.

"Ah, sir," she said, "if you can bear up a moment longer . . ."

Quickly she delved into a cupboard, brought out a glass, and poured a generous portion of brandy into it. Then, seating herself beside him, she raised the goblet gently to his lips and allowed a tiny sip to run into his mouth.

"Mmmm," he sighed. "Life is stirrin' in me veins."

She raised the glass again. After a comfortable pause she raised it again, and then again, offering the liquid to him sip by sip. He allowed her to minister to him for a time, but finally he took the glass gently from her fingers and tipped the remainder into his mouth.

"Ambrosia," he breathed. "A darlin' man, is Barleycorn. If you'll offer me another portion o' the same, I'll not say nay, and I'll be as right as rain in a twinklin'."

"But, sir," she protested, "it is extremely strong spirits I have given you. You must not drink it down as though it were water. I fear your system will receive a dreadful shock."

"No, no, kind lady," he assured her. "In times o' anguish a shock is precisely what the system requires. Another dose o' spirits is the medicine I need to put me right. Any physician will tell you so."

"Oh," she said, frowning. "Very well."

She rose and poured another generous measure into the glass. When she handed it back to him, he downed half in a hearty swallow, then relaxed against the cushions with a sigh and sat turning the goblet slowly in his hand, first one way and then the other, while he gazed ruminatively into its amber depths.

"Poor Tristam," he murmured. "Poor cherished lad. That he should come to grief in this house

. . ." He sighed heavily. "I predicted t'would be so, but I'd not expected nemesis to show herself in this disguise."

"Nor I, sir," Callie agreed. "Who could have known that it would be an innocent bystander who would suffer calamity at my parents' hands?"

They sat for a moment with their heads bowed, musing on the capriciousness of fate. Then both turned slightly to cast a sidelong glance at each other. The gentleman's color had improved, and Callie was surprised to note that he was much younger than she had at first believed. In fact, she wondered if he were not, perhaps, only a few years older than Brandy, for despite the ravages which dissipation had wrought around his eyes, his brow was smooth and unlined.

"If you will permit me, sir," she ventured, "in view of the unusual circumstances prevailing at this time, I shall not await a proper introduction but shall instead present myself to you. I am Carolyn Belcroft."

He nodded. "And I . . ." He sprang to his feet and executed a sprightly little schottische, then made an elaborate leg. "Tristam's cousin, Morgan Troville Percival Fenn, at your service."

"Oh," she said, momentarily disconcerted by his capering. "Yes . . . I see. Indeed, it is a pleasure to meet you. Won't you be seated, please?"

"Thank you." He sat down again beside her and, picking up his glass from the small side table where he had set it, tossed off the remainder of the cognac and held the empty goblet out to her again. She pretended not to see it.

"I am sorry Brandy is away," she began. "He would be able to tell you precisely what Sir Neville has predicted concerning your cousin's recovery."

To her surprise there was a stentorian sob from Fenn, and his shoulders began to shake again.

"Oh, dear sir!" she protested.

He held his handkerchief to his eyes. "Forgive me. 'Tis an agony t' see 'im sufferin', so like a son he always was to me."

"A son?" she said. "How can you say so, sir, when you and Lord Tristam are nearly of an age?"

"No, no!" he insisted. "Much younger, he is. Much, much younger. An' many's the time I carried 'im about on me shoulders when he was a wee lad. Across a stream at flood tide once. I remember it well." He chuckled and wiped at his eyes. "Clung t' me head so's I could scarcely see, the scamp. Almost sent us into the Mergot's Hole and lost forever."

"My goodness!" Callie breathed. She pressed a hand to her cheek. Fenn, she noted, was gazing longingly at his empty glass. Experiencing a sudden pang of remorse, she picked it up and refilled it. "Thank heaven you were spared!" she said, passing it back to him.

"Aye," he agreed, downing a hearty draught. "That were a near thing—me staggerin' about wi' the lad on me neck an' him grittin' 'is teeth t' keep from screechin'. Heart like a lion, that little one; never accused o' showin' the white feather, I can assure you." He chuckled happily to himself and took another pull at his brandy.

"What a wonderful relationship," Callie said. "It

190

must indeed give you pain to see him suffering as he is at this time."

"Aye," Fenn agreed, draining his glass. "Dreadful, it is."

His eyes filled with tears and, wiping them with his handkerchief, he passed the goblet back to Callie. With another sigh he rose unsteadily to his feet. "I'll be on me way, lass. At White's there'll be a game to woo me thoughts away from the little shaver."

"Indeed, sir," Callie told him. "Be assured that Sir Neville has nothing but the highest hopes for Lord Tristam's recovery."

"Ah," he said, "that thought'll keep me from the depths o' despair." But despite his words, he went out through the door, his head deeply bowed.

After he had departed, Callie remained where she was, musing. Vivid pictures flashed through her mind—of Tristam as a little child pattering doglike in the footsteps of the older man. When she remembered Fenn's description of the drama near Mergot's Hole, a coldness took possession of her. She was clasping and unclasping her hands, endeavoring to put a train of morbid thoughts from her mind, when the door opened and Brandy walked in.

"Ah, popsy, here you are," he said. "You must tidy yourself for dinner. Cook tells me we have a baron of beef and some of those meringues you're so fond of."

Callie rose slowly to her feet. "The most astonishing man came here today to visit Tristam," she told him. "His name is Morgan Fenn."

"Ah, yes, good old Morg," Brandy said, his face

relaxing into a smile. "I hear he has become astonishing indeed!"

"I could have wept for him," she went on. "He was utterly devastated by Tristam's suffering."

"Really? That doesn't sound like Morg."

"But it is natural when one considers that Tristam has always been like a son to him."

Brandy laughed. "A son! How is that possible when there is only three years between them?"

Callie's mouth sagged open. "I believe you are mistaken, Brandy. He distinctly stated that he used to carry Tristam about on his shoulders, and he referred to him as 'the lad.' "

"Nonsense!" Brandy snorted. "I've known Morgan most of my life; I know precisely how old he is. And carry Tristam about, never! Such a great hulking giant Tris was as a child!" He frowned. "Is it possible poor Fenn is in worse shape than I had realized?"

"I dare say he is very ill," Callie said. "He told me the most fanciful tales—about a thrilling rescue in which he saved Tristam's life from a raging torrent and they both nearly went to their deaths in a thing called Mergot's Hole."

"Well, that's true enough," Brandy admitted. "Morg always was a prodigious swimmer; Tris fell into a river somewhere, and Fenn dove in after him. They were nearly swept into a hole in the rocks where the water goes down and comes out in the sea some twenty miles farther on."

"How remarkable," Callie said. "But since Mr.

Fenn was truly a hero, why should he lie about the rest?"

Brandy shook his head slowly. "I don't know. I've no idea how things have been going with him over the years; but it's a well known fact that he likes his spirits." He frowned suddenly. "He hadn't shot the cat before he called here, had he?"

Callie's cheeks flushed. "Well, no," she said. "Not before he arrived, I don't believe."

Brandy looked at her curiously. "How was he when he left?"

"A bit tipsy," she admitted.

Her brother scowled. "And how did he get that way? You didn't give him liquor, surely, Cal?"

"Well, I did," she explained. "He was so shaken and frail, I gave him something to revive him."

Brandy snorted. "Frail, indeed! He was always strong as an ox; and I can't believe he's fallen on such evil times, since Tristam watches out for him. No, Callie, you've stepped out of line. You'd no business serving spirits to any man. In fact, you should not have received him while you were alone in the house."

"But I did not," she protested. "I found him in the hall outside Tristam's door, barely able to stand."

Brandy let out a bark of laughter. "I wish I'd seen him, the cunning rascal." He pondered for a moment, then frowned. "I wonder if Fenn's a bit touched in his upper works."

Callie was silent. She ran a finger tentatively over her lips. "Brandy," she said slowly, "is Tristam an object of ridicule because of his cousin?"

"No, no," her brother said, "certainly not!"

"Then it is possible that other families—other than ours, I mean—have members who are a bit, well, *eccentric?*"

He nodded. "Every family. That is why you must not be so goosish about your sleepwalking. In fact, I have given it some thought and have decided that it will be very easy for you to control it, if you will—just as Fenn could control his bouts with demon rum. You need only sit down in a chair several minutes before retiring and say over and over to yourself, 'I shall not walk! I shall not walk!' I was talking to Boobie Chappell this afternoon, and he told me of a fellow who did that very thing and rid himself of hiccups."

"Oh, Brandy," she protested, "that will accomplish nothing, I swear."

"It will work, I am positive," he insisted. "And you must put your mind to it this very evening, for I am too exhausted to chase you over the rooftops all night. Come now, popsy, you can do it if you will."

Callie took a deep breath and exhaled. "Very well," she said, nodding solemnly. "I shall try."

By evening Regina was resting comfortably and felt sufficiently improved to partake of a light meal. Tristam, on the other hand, was suffering more pain than ever, and when Sir Neville visited him, he administered another substantial dose of laudanum. It was not long thereafter that the marquis sank into a profound but troubled slumber.

He discovered that the laudanum masked rather

than relieved his pain. He was never quite free from the deep throbbing ache that beat constantly through his leaden arm, working its way steadily across his shoulder and into his spine; and it was not long before the drug had caused his consciousness to wander. He found himself wafting along an undulating trail of whispering sensations into an eerie world of fantasy. First he was aware of muffled sounds within Belcroft House—servants' feet marching across the cellars, other feet scurrying in the upper regions, and the occasional murmur of hushed voices. Then he imagined he was on the banks of a turbulent river. His aching arm hung flaccid and ponderous at his side while he watched the currents surge over hidden rocks and melt into shimmering colors. There were fingers of canary yellow and eddies of azure blue, and they were sliding over layers of viscous red blood.

His heart surged at the sight of that erubescent fluid and for a moment pounded violently against his ribs. Then it slowed, and he felt himself sinking backward into a clutching softness. Around him the water was rising out of its bed and swirling into coils of brilliantly hued flowers.

He was watching a pinwheel of whirling marigolds when he felt a rush of cooler air; and to his surprise a white figure with both arms outstretched came drifting past him. Her hair was blowing softly around her face, like a plume of yellow flame.

"Callie," he whispered.

The phantom paused and turned toward him.

"I shall not walk . . ." she whispered. "I shall not walk . . ."

"Callie," he tried again; but this time he could not pull the word out of the swollen pocket of hot cotton wool that was his mouth.

To his surprise he saw that her face was coming toward him, hovering over his bed. He tried to reach out his healthy arm and pull her close to him, but he had grown so heavy that every part of him weighed more than a ton and would not stir.

If only I could hold her, he thought. *If only I could feel her body pressed against me, every tribulation would melt away.*

But he was unable to move. Her mouth was descending slowly; he waited, holding his breath. Then her lips touched his in a long trembling kiss, and he felt the world drop away beneath him.

"Good God, you wretched girl!" Brandy cried, towing his sister relentlessly by the wrist as he strode furiously along the corridor. "What sort of infamy are you trying to bring down upon this house, wandering into men's bedrooms at night and kissing them in their sleep? Let us hope that Tristam was unconscious—or believes himself to have been indulging in a fanciful dream."

Callie, who was stumbling along behind him as fast as she could, tried to pull back but was jerked forward so hard that she was obliged to execute several steps of a Highland fling to keep from being thrown to her knees. "But I didn't intend . . ." she began.

He stopped and turned on her furiously. "*Didn't intend!* What if you had leaned on his arm—had broken it again? By God, I've been too patient with you—and I have been too patient with our parents! From now on I shall not coddle any of you. I shall treat you all as roughly as you deserve. If you walk again, miss, instead of gently leading you back to your bed, I shall grasp you by the shoulders and shake you until your teeth rattle! I shall shake you awake, and if it gives you a shock, then perhaps you will think twice before you wander off again. By heaven, this very night I shall tie your ankle to the bedpost, and if you try to creep about, you'll crash to the floor. That will end this nonsensical behavior once and for all!"

Thoroughly chastened, Callie allowed her brother to shove her back into her room and slam the door loudly behind her. Stumbling to her bed, she threw herself full length upon it and gave herself up to wracking sobs.

Brandy arose shortly after noon the next day and made his way, leaden-eyed, to the breakfast table. He found his mother seated there, toying with a bit of roll which she was dabbing absentmindedly in a blob of marmalade. At sight of him her face instantly wreathed itself in smiles.

"Ah, my dearest," she caroled. "How delightful to find you here. I am feeling so much more the thing since that villain retired to Colter Abbey. Let us have a party—perhaps twenty couples; and I may engage Mr. Keene to read some poems to us."

Brandy frowned. "I think that will not be possible,

Mama. We must preserve the utmost quiet in order to hasten Tristam's recovery, and I fear he will still be mending for the next week or two."

"Bother!" she exclaimed. "But certainly it is not necessary to creep about in this ridiculous hushed way and keep our voices at a funereal level for an entire week. I have finally rid myself of that detestable Osgood—foolish, cruel, implacable man—and now, instead of enjoying myself with a few simple pleasures, I must tiptoe and whisper in my own house because we are burdened with a great hulking invalid."

"Mama!" he protested. "I cannot believe I am hearing you rightly. It was your prank which put him where he is. The very least we can do is care for him the best way we are able and with good grace. Even that cannot begin to compensate him for what he is suffering."

"No, no," she objected, "it was Osgood's persecution which drove me to retaliate. And I am most dreadfully sorry that Tristam was the victim. But I cannot sit about in this silent, brooding house and make myself gray and hagged with remorse. I shall go out for some entertainment tonight. First I'll join the Markhams at a small dinner party, and then perhaps I'll go to the theater with Lord Blessfield— he was one of my most ardent suitors before I chose your father, and Helena Markham made a special point of mentioning that she had also invited him." Her eyes began to sparkle as she leaned toward her son and gave him an affectionate kiss on the cheek.

"Do not overtax yourself, my dear," she urged. "I

realize that you gave your word to guard your sister from harm; but you are looking extremely weary today. If she is becoming too much of a burden, send her back to Colter Abbey."

"No," Brandy said, shaking his head. "I am still convinced that she will stop walking as soon as she is happy. But things have indeed become more critical than I had anticipated, and I've had grills put over her bedroom windows—as at home—and the doorknobs removed."

"Yes, yes," Regina agreed. "That is undoubtedly wise."

"And," he continued, "I wonder if we should not make an effort to promote a match for her as quickly as possible. Who shall the lucky man be, Tristam or Rowan?" He was thoughtful for a moment. "Perhaps Ro would be the better choice; he's healthy at the moment, and he's kindhearted, good-natured, charming, and rich. What more could any girl require?"

Regina shrugged. "Certainly he sounds the perfect mate. I give the match my blessing. And I suggest . . ."

But before she could complete her recommendation, Seffronia stormed into the room, puffing and snorting with indignation.

"Indeed!" she cried. "To what may we attribute this latest atrocity? I was never so shocked in my life as when I approached the front of this house! Those gratings over Callie's windows are plainly visible from the street, and they present the grimmest, most sinister appearance imaginable. You must instantly contrive to disguise them, for at present they proclaim to the world that Belcroft House is in fact a prison, or perhaps even Bedlam Hospital."

"Good God!" Regina exclaimed. "They must be covered before Gracia comes to visit Tristam." She turned to her butler. "Rimpson, we must set Mrs. Halloway to work at once putting curtains between the gratings and the windows of Miss Callie's room. Lady Gracia will be calling on us at any moment."

"Begging your ladyship's pardon," Rimpson explained, "but the Marchioness of Waivering has already paid her visit—some time ago, in fact—and has departed, bearing the marquis away with her."

"What!" Regina shrieked. "Why was I not wakened to receive her?"

Rimpson's face stiffened. "I endeavored to rouse your ladyship and Master Brandon but was informed at the time—quite emphatically, I might add—that you did not wish to be disturbed for any reason."

Brandy and Regina gaped at each other.

"Such incivility!" Seffronia clucked. "Gracia should be ashamed of herself."

"But surely I did not tell you with my own lips that I did not wish to be disturbed," Brandy challenged his butler.

"Begging your pardon, sir," Rimpson informed him, "you did, indeed."

"Well, of all the abominable coils!" Brandy muttered. He turned to his mother. "Why were you so deep in the arms of Morpheus, Mama, after all the sleep you had yesterday?"

"I have no idea," she admitted. "Unless it was the

drop of laudanum I took last night to complete my recovery and guarantee that I should be in my very best looks today. But I shall never forgive Gracia for this, the sly minx. I swear I have never been so offended in my entire life."

"Let us wait until we know the reasons behind her curious behavior," Brandy suggested. "I cannot believe Tris would be such a johnny raw as to leave us without a word. There must be other circumstances of which we know nothing."

Regina and Seffronia wagged their eyebrows at each other knowingly.

Late in the afternoon Brandy took a turn around the park on a new hack, and before he returned home, he rode to Waivering House and stopped to check on Tristam's progress. He was greeted, to his surprise, by a silent building with the shutters up and the knocker removed. On circling the house and banging on a rear door, he managed to raise the caretaker, who, with a peevish scowl, came out into the passageway, muttering sullenly at the intrusion.

"No, sir," he said, with a minimum effort at civility, " 'is lordship is not at 'ome. 'Er ladyship took 'im orf to Marcourt where 'e'll be safe 'n' sound."

"It is certainly the strangest thing," Rowan agreed when he heard of the Waiverings' flight. "Don't see how the marchioness could have been so uncivil. I mean, dash it all, she's not noted for being a loose screw."

Brandy nodded. "What I would like to know is

precisely what she said to Tris to get him to agree. That would make my task much simpler."

"Your task?" Rowan asked him in surprise. "What task would that be, old man?"

Brandy stared silently off into space. "Do you think she might have heard rumors about Callie?" he asked, taking another tack.

"Rumors?" Rowan exclaimed, starting violently. "Certainly not! What sort of rumors could she have heard? There are no rumors."

"Oh, but there are," Brandy corrected him. "That is one thing I do know."

"You do?" Rowan said, surprised. "Then you realize it would explain Lady Gracia's catching Tris up and running off with him—if he had indicated in some way that he might be losing his heart to your sister. I mean, a mother might worry about such things."

Brandy began to pace back and forth across the room. "But that is the thing! There is no cause to take flight. Callie's affliction is not serious. It is the result of the strain placed on her nerves by my mother and father's constant quarrels."

Rowan peered at him eagerly. "It is not hereditary?"

"Good God, no!" Brandy assured him. "She was the most normal little thing in the world when she was a child. Of course, my parents' squabbles were milder then. It was not until they began to fight so viciously that she was deeply affected."

"Well, by Jove!" Rowan exclaimed. "If that is the

case, tranquility and happiness should bring about a cure."

"I am confident they will."

"Then let us apply ourselves to entertaining her," Rowan urged. "I should be happy to spend every waking hour in her company, if it will be of benefit."

Chapter 15

When evening approached without bringing a letter from Tristam or his mother, Brandy seated himself at his desk and applied himself to the task of writing to his friend. He informed him that he hoped he was not suffering excessive discomfort. He also expressed regret that he had been asleep at the time of Tristam's departure and therefore deprived of the satisfaction of bidding him farewell—it was necessary for him to rewrite this passage several times before he was satisfied that there was no hint of censure implied. Then he concluded by hoping that he would be able to enjoy his friend's company again soon. Having completed his missive and sealed it with a wafer, he called one of his footmen, mounted the man on a sturdy hack, and sent him off to Marcourt to deliver the letter in person.

The man returned two hours later and reported that he had not seen the marquis, his lordship having been sequestered in his room. But he had delivered the letter to Lady Gracia herself.

On the following day everyone noted a marked decline in Callie's spirits. Her cheeks were perceptibly paler, and her movements had a listlessness which could only be attributed to profound dejection.

Although the windows of her bedroom had been hung with curtains which effectively hid the gratings, whispers had begun to circulate anew among the ton, and the few members of Society who had remained in town found activities and duties which made it necessary for them to decline all invitations to Belcroft House. While Regina busied herself with numerous entertainments, she also began to grow wan and irritable.

"It's this wretched heat!" she told her sister one morning when Seffronia was taking a cup of tea with her. "What ever induced me to remain in town during these months I shall never know. I would give the remainder of my life for one clean breath of fresh country air."

Seffronia watched her thoughtfully. "Is it truly the heat, my love, or is it lack of interesting companionship and the strain of Callie's unhappiness?"

"Well, I don't know, I'm sure," she admitted. "But I am certain that if the girl continues to wander about the house in this drooping manner, meeting me at every turn with that gloomy face, I shall be obliged to flee for my life. I have told Brandy that he must find a way to cheer her!"

That evening Brandy made his first concerted effort to raise his sister's spirits when he brought home a small shaggy puppy and presented it to her. It was a round ball of fur which bounced all over the vestibule floor, falling over its paws and drawing crows of delight from Callie when it repeatedly stumbled over its chin whiskers and sprawled onto its stomach.

"Oh, Brandy!" she cried. "Is it possible that anything so tiny can be truly alive?"

"Such an amusing little chap," Regina laughed. "Ha, ha, little fellow! No, no, bad boy, do not jump at my skirt; you'll tear my gown with those sharp little claws."

"Oh, dear," Callie exclaimed, "he is so wriggly I shall never be able to hold him without dropping him." She burst into trills of laughter as he skidded in circles around her. "Where are his eyes?"

Brandy caught up the puppy in a hand and, holding him close to his sister's face, brushed back the mop of unruly hair to reveal two huge, moist, black, buttonlike orbs.

"Oh." She drew in her breath. "Poor little creature. Have you ever seen such an unhappy expression on a puppy's face?"

"Nonsense!" Brandy protested. "He's a bright, cheerful, alert little beast. He has come to amuse you." And with a quick movement he set the puppy on the floor at Callie's feet. "There!" he commanded. "Run in a circle and make my sister laugh!"

But the dog promptly collapsed and rolled onto its back. Raising both its hind legs in the air, it lay trembling.

"Here, here, now," Regina scolded, pushing gently at it with her toe. "Get up, you little imp and dance for us."

"Perhaps," Seffronia suggested, "he is unhappy because his eyes are covered with hair."

"He is not unhappy!" Brandy roared.

Alarmed by the stridor of his master's voice, the dog rolled onto its side and crawled along the floor until it was able to take refuge behind Callie's feet. There it peered out at Brandy anxiously and ducked its head as though expecting a blow.

"He's afraid of you," Callie said.

"Good God!" Brandy protested. "If you will dwell on pathos in this ridiculous manner and cannot even enjoy the foolish capering of a happy little dog, I wash my hands of you all."

He gave a snort of indignation and marched out of the room. Regina, already weary of the puppy's antics, followed him. Callie and Seffronia for some time thereafter endeavored to coax the puppy back to its previous giddy state, but with only moderate success.

"I am convinced his spirits are dampened by that mop of hair over his eyes," Seffronia told her niece. "If we could trim it so that he might see, he will certainly feel more lively."

Making their way into the yellow saloon, Callie and her aunt extracted a pair of embroidery scissors from Regina's work basket and endeavored to liberate the puppy's eyes. He jumped and wriggled and whined so vehemently, however, that they soon began to fear they would blind him, and abandoned their effort after exposing one eye. This amused them for a time, the aunt and niece laughing together at the confidential winks the puppy appeared to be giving them; but soon Callie's spirits sagged again, and the puppy's mood immediately reflected hers. The following morning when Brandy observed the drooping figure of his sister trailing into the breakfast room with the wilted little dog following silently in her wake, its ears flat and its tail down, he retreated in consternation to Rowan Dillworth's house.

"There must be something we can do to bring her out of her mopes," he exclaimed, punching one of his fists into his other palm. "I cannot understand why she is so obdurate in her melancholy."

"Perhaps," Rowan suggested, "she would find amusement at the theater. There is a delightful comedy at the Swan, I am told. It may be the very thing to bring her spirits around."

"Indeed it may!" Brandy agreed. "I have never failed to be cheered by a rollicking comedy."

It appeared that they had at last found a solution to the problem when that evening Callie addressed herself with interest to the play and even began to smile at certain bits of nonsense in the first act. But then, to her companions' horror, the hero strode onto the stage and proved to be a large young man with black hair who bore a striking resemblance to Waivering; and for reasons necessary to the plot he carried one arm in a sling. Glancing quickly at his sister, Brandy saw that his worst fears were realized; her lips had begun to quiver.

Later, when this same hero involved himself in a swordfight, Callie squeaked and wrung her hands, and when the villain, with a spate of highly amusing asides, ran the young man through and left him expiring center stage amidst the delighted laughter of the rest of the audience, Callie sobbed and hiccuped so piteously that Brandy was obliged to hurry her out of the theater and march her back and forth through a nearby park until she had regained some small degree of composure.

Toward the end of September the heat lay heavily over the city. Most genteel entertainments had been suspended, although Regina found activities to occupy her every night and spent her days browsing restlessly through the shops. Seffronia sometimes accompanied her on her excursions, though more often she aided Brandy and Rowan in their attempts to cheer Callie and ease her mind. These efforts proved singularly unsuccessful.

They visited the Elgin Marbles, which Callie characterized as "interesting." They spent a day at the Tower, which Callie found "stark," and three days at the British Museum, which she dubbed "educational," with the result that the girl grew daily more weary, silent, and pale. Their most successful excursion was to Vauxhall Gardens, where they enjoyed a boat ride across the river and partook of a delicious meal, then attended the Grand Cascade. This spectacle brought a smile to Callie's lips, the first Brandy and Rowan had been able to coax from her in some time. Shortly thereafter, however, they were the victims of an unfortunate incident.

Young Viscount Puddingleigh, a friend of both Brandy's and Rowan's, was lounging comfortably against a tree trunk as the Belcroft party strolled by. Catching sight of Callie, he straightened up, stared at her in wonder, his mouth sagging open, and called to a friend who was chatting with another beau behind him, "My God, Aubrey, turn around and look at this girl! Have you ever seen such an exquisite creature?"

His companion, however, quickly caught hold of his wrist and pulled him back toward the shelter of some shrubs. "Shhh," he hissed. "That's Callie Belcroft."

Puddingleigh's eyes opened wider. "What a pity!" he said; and without a word to either Rowan or Brandy he slipped quickly away into a grove of trees behind him.

Brandy, seething with indignation, hoped Callie had not overheard; but when he looked at his sister's face, he saw that tears were welling out of her eyes, and a moment later they were running freely down her cheeks.

Chapter 16

The following morning Rowan visited the Belcrofts at his usual hour and found Seffronia in consultation with Regina and Brandy.

"Ah, here you are, Ro," Brandy greeted him. "We have decided to take Callie back to the abbey. It is apparent that I am doing her nothing but harm here. Poor creature, I heard her footsteps all through the night. I doubt that she was able to lie quietly an hour through, in consequence of that dashed Puddingleigh's outrageous behavior."

Rowan clicked his tongue sympathetically. "But to return her to Colter Abbey, Brandy . . . I wish you would not. I have wondered these past few days if a trip to Meadowmere might not have a beneficial effect upon her nerves."

"Dear, dear," Seffronia clucked. "Why should you wish to burden yourself with our problems, Mr. Dillworth?"

Rowan's round cheeks flushed. "It would be the greatest pleasure for me, ma'am, to have all of you as my guests. Lady Regina"—he bowed deeply to her—"you once indicated that you would not be averse to tendering a bit of advice on my gardens. And I should think that you would all be better equipped than I am myself to make decisions on the architectural experiments I should attempt. Miss Callie would perhaps also find the building interesting and have some notions as to how I might improve the place."

"Oh, I don't think she would," Brandy said. "She has never been interested in building ruined chapels and follies and things of that sort."

"My dearest," Seffronia protested, casting him a speaking look, "I am confident you are mistaken. She has expressed the liveliest interest in Meadowmere. It will be a delightful new experience for her, I collect, to visit such a place; and the tranquility of the countryside will certainly have a soothing effect upon us all."

"Yes, yes, you must agree," Rowan urged. He turned to Regina. "And you know, ma'am, that Lord Blessfield's seat marches with mine. We shall entice him to join us for a small dinner party, if the prospect pleases you."

"Blessfield!" Regina snorted indignantly. "Such a buffoon! Spare me, sir, I beg of you! I had forgotten the reasons for my rejection of him years ago, and now I find—even more than then—I cannot abide the foolish creature."

"It shall be just our own little group then," Rowan suggested. "A delightful party during the waning days of summer. What could be more restful?"

Seffronia managed to catch Brandy's eye and wag her eyebrows expressively at him. He looked at her curiously for a moment; then, as he realized her intent, his own brows rose.

"Yes, yes," he agreed rather more loudly than necessary. "Delightful notion, Ro. We should all enjoy a visit to Meadowmere. It will certainly be the very thing to put us back into fine fettle."

Later, when he was alone with his aunt, he applauded her cunning. "You were right to urge this trip," he told her. "If we are clever and diligent, we shall be able to fix Callie's affections firmly on Rowan. Such an excellent fellow!"

"It is all a matter of persistence and the right atmosphere," Seffronia agreed. "Callie will soon abandon any tendre she might have felt for Tristam when she considers what rudeness the Waiverings have displayed."

Brandy frowned and for a moment stared thoughtfully off into space. "I should like to know precisely what has transpired with the Waiverings—what sort of machinations are being practiced, and by whom. This whole episode is so unlike Tris. I have written him three letters and have not received even one reply; and when I consider the closeness of our relationship and the days he has spent under my roof, I find it difficult to believe that he has turned his back on me so irrevocably."

"I am confident that your friendship is at an end until Callie is safely married," Seffronia told him. "I would wager the remainder of my life that Gracia is the villain in this piece; I have written her twice, myself, and received no answer—and when you realize how much longer her friendship and mine

. . . Well, there is no profit in repining."

"So, if it is Gracia who has caused this schism," Brandy continued, "what is to be done?"

"Nothing," Seffronia told him. "You cannot beard the lioness in her den; and it is quite plain to me that she will spare no effort to defend her cub."

From the many stories Callie had heard about Meadowmere, she expected to behold a country mansion of breathtaking proportions with classic lines and ornate formal gardens. Instead she found a rather squat house of monotonous gray stone with an odd-shaped Gothic tower on its southeast corner and bits of scaffolding set about in unexpected places. In front of the main section was a long, rectangular pond which appeared oddly out of place, reflecting little more than the slate-gray monotony of a hazy sky.

"Well, dear me," Seffronia said to Regina and Callie in the privacy of their carriage as they approached the edifice, "I never thought Meadowmere more than a nondescript pile of granite, and I fear poor dear Rowan will not be able to turn it into a silk purse after all."

"It is certainly not handsome," Callie agreed. "What shall we say to our host when he asks our opinion?"

"Tell him the truth," Regina grumbled. She was sitting slouched in a corner of the carriage, her brow rumpled in a sullen scowl. "Say it is ugly and hopeless and you are eager to leave it."

"My dear, my dear!" Seffronia protested. "You

214

know you will do no such thing yourself. The moment dear Rowan receives you, you will go out of your way to be charming to him."

"Yes, yes," her sister admitted. "There is no harm in the lad—I have always been fond of him—and I shall let him know that we appreciate his kindness. But I am not confident I can retain my good humor much longer if this weather does not change. This heat and dust are unbearable! If you will remember, this is the time of year when Osgood always becomes restless and does foolish things which endanger his safety. Wherever he is, he will probably ride neck or nothing over a wall somewhere and kill himself, as Ansel did, the clodpoll!"

Seffronia clicked her tongue. "Why should Osgood come to mind, my love? Do you suppose your malaise is brought about by loneliness; is it possible you miss him?"

"Good God!" Regina cried. "What an outrageous suggestion! How can you chaff me so heartlessly? I never wish to hear his name again!"

While Regina did not flourish at Meadowmere, Callie began to show signs of recovery the moment a breath of fresh country air wafted over her. The first morning of her stay she rode forth with Rowan to enjoy a long gallop over the verdant fields. She was mounted on a white Arabian mare which her host had recently procured from a business associate in the Middle East, and as Rowan galloped alongside her on a glossy bay hack, he was pleased to note that some color was already returning to her cheeks.

They rode briskly down a long sloping meadow, then into a lane which wound its way among Rowan's farms, and for several minutes loped contentedly side by side until they passed beyond a cypress hedge and came out alongside a small cottage that had a kitchen garden beside it. There a barefooted young woman in a faded dress was weeding her vegetables. Behind her a ragged child of less than a year sat in the middle of a spaded patch, stuffing bits of dirt into its mouth.

The woman rose quickly from her knees and dropped a curtsy in her master's direction; but when she saw Callie's expression of horror, she turned quickly to the child and discovered his mischief. With a gasp she slapped the dirt from his hands. Immediately the baby let out a shriek and began to scream at the top of his lungs. Sweeping him up in her arms, the mother wiped the mud from his lips and began to purr to him.

"There, there, little love," she murmured. "D' no' cry, precious darlin'." She pressed her cheek against his, but he flailed furiously with his fists and screamed into her ear. Rowan and Callie passed on, rounding another corner of the lane and moving into the shelter of an ancient stone wall.

"Well!" Rowan exclaimed, his face pink with indignation. "No wonder these laborers' children are so dashed unhealthy, eating dirt and who-knows-what-else. And being knocked about by their mothers, they are bound to become hardened and insensible. If I am to improve their conditions for them, I must first . . ." But before he could finish, he caught sight of his companion's face and discovered to his surprise that her eyes were full of tears. "My dear Miss Belcroft!" he protested. "Whatever can be the matter?"

Callie sniffled. "If only I were that woman instead of myself," she mourned. "How I envy her!"

"Good God!" he cried. "How can you say such a thing! She is only a poor laborer's wife, while you are the daughter of a peer; she is only a simple, plain-faced creature, while you are a great beauty; she is without talent, education . . . indeed, without any future but the grave, while you are a lady of the utmost refinement, charm, delicacy . . . destined, no doubt, to fill one of the highest positions in the land . . . respected, admired . . . yes, even adored!"

His face grew pink with emotion; and as he looked at her, realizing that everything he said was true, it was borne in upon him what a truly splendid and desirable creature she was. He observed the limpid eyes still spilling tears, and the delicate arching throat, so frail and vulnerable. This exquisite, fragile girl, so in need of protection . . . His heart swelled within him.

"My dear Miss Belcroft," he began in a voice that was suddenly gravelly and unsteady, "we have been acquainted but a short time. I realize that I am being presumptuous. I can never be worthy, of that I am too much aware . . . but I feel impelled to speak. My dearest . . . er . . . Callie . . . will you do me the great . . . the undeserved . . . but infinitely desired . . . the honor . . ." He broke off, overcome by the intensity of his feelings.

217

Callie peered at him apprehensively out of the corner of her eye. "Sir," she protested, "I beg of you; do not continue."

"I must!" he went on. "You do not realize . . . that is . . . if you could consider . . . if . . . the great honor . . . well, that is . . . er . . . becoming my wife." He broke off, flushing a violent red.

She raised a gloved hand and fluttered it in front of her face. "Please, sir!" she said. "You have not considered. I can not marry *anyone*."

"How can you say so?" he exclaimed. "You would make *anyone* the happiest of men!"

With a frantic shake of her head she snapped the reins against her horse's neck and galloped away. Perplexed, Rowan sat watching her retreating back.

"Shy little thing," he murmured to himself. "Hasn't had time to realize I'm offering her Meadowmere and more wealth than anyone could ever need."

It occurred to him that he should have made his position clear on the matter of property rights and marriage settlements and the like—though he had been under the impression that those things should be discussed with the girl's father and not be allowed to detract from the romance of the occasion—but if there were some question in her mind as to what, precisely, her situation would be . . .

Ah, well, he thought, *we shall see.* With a shake of his head he pressed his knees into his horse's sides and cantered slowly back to the stable.

She had long since disappeared by the time he reached the house, and he made his way to the library and sat down at his desk to patiently await her reappearance. He was thumbing restlessly through a new shipment of books when Brandy put his head in the door.

"Ah, Ro, you are here," he said, entering and settling himself into a deep leather chair. He peered at him curiously. "Look a bit megrimish, if I may say so."

"Yes, yes," Rowan agreed. "I've been a gapeseed, Brandy. Not the right thing—should have got your permission, and all that, since your father's not here —but got carried away and proposed to your sister before I thought what I was about."

"Well!" Brandy exclaimed. "Couldn't be more delighted! No doubt she said yes."

"That's just the thing; she ran off, and I've not the slightest clue as to whether she intends to accept me or not."

Brandy frowned. "I've no doubt she will, when she's had time to consider."

"But don't you see?" his host explained. "I had expected her to take me up in an instant, what with all the material advantages I'm able to offer her; but I've the strongest impression that she intends to decline. In fact, decline *all* offers she might receive."

Brandy sighed heavily. "This is such a dashed perplexing business! Damned if I know where it will end."

"Perhaps if I exhibit patience," Rowan suggested.

Brandy nodded. "It can do no harm, at any rate."

"I have had no experience with women," Rowan

said. "I do not have the faintest notion how to begin to influence one."

"On the other hand," Brandy told him, "I know them quite well, and I do not have the faintest notion how to influence one either."

They were busily discussing the unpredictability of the female sex when Foster entered the room to announce the arrival of a young gentleman in a sporting curricle.

"Viscount Landborough, sir," he explained. "The same who spent a week with us here in the spring—and, if I may take the liberty of reminding you, sir, broke the Ming vase when he attempted to balance it on his nose. Perhaps you would wish me to inform him that you are not at home?"

"No, no!" Rowan exclaimed, brightening. "Show him in." He turned to Brandy. "It's dear old Chipper. You remember him from Eton. Always ate walnuts in bed after the lights were out and then was deuced hard put to get rid of the shells."

"Good God!" Brandy breathed. "Old Chipper! Does he still have that wriggly pink nose and rabbity chin?"

But Viscount Landborough's chin had long since disappeared behind an elegant Vandyke goatee, and his little black mustache gave him a striking resemblance to a well-known portrait of Sir Walter Raleigh. He was ushered into Rowan's study and, after being thumped soundly on the back by both young gentlemen, was urged into a large comfortable chair and plied with refreshing beverages.

"Mmmm, delicious," he murmured, pulling at his

glass. "This is a devilish sight better stuff than I received at Marcourt. Tristam is a good fellow and all that, but he does not know the first thing about wine."

"Tristam?" Rowan exclaimed. "You've seen him?"

"Yes, spent the past few nights there. I'm junketing about the country, you see, spending a few days here and a few days there with old friends, trying to kill time until my mother leaves Landborough Place to visit my sister in Bath. Been making my life miserable the past few weeks; taken it into her head that I must find a bride and produce an heir—duty to the family and all that sort of rot. If there's one thing I do not intend to do, it's leg shackle myself to some peagoose with a pretty face and fallaway airs who'll put a spoke in my wheel just when the hunting season's getting underway."

"How is Tristam's arm?" Brandy interrupted.

"Coming along," Landborough told him. "Out of the cast and all that, but it gives him a twinge now and then. That reminds me—I'm glad to find you here, Brandy, as I've a message for you which I should undoubtedly have forgotten by the time I met you in town."

"A message from Tris?" Brandy asked in great excitement.

"Yes. He wants to know what the devil you're thinking of to ignore his letters as you do? With all the years you've been friends, he feels that you owe him a reply, no matter how disgusted with him you might be."

"Disgusted!" Brandy's face grew pink with indignation. "Indeed I am! I have written three letters which he has not taken the trouble to answer. Do I not have the right to be disgusted, I ask you?"

"But he claims that he has written you two letters —very laboriously produced while his arm was still useless—and has not received one in return. He warns you that as soon as he is able to ride any distance, he is going to come looking for you and give you a thorough drubbing."

Rowan and Brandy exchanged solemn glances.

"Skulduggery," Rowan observed.

Brandy nodded.

Chapter 17

The ladies, still recovering from their long journey of the previous day, declined to appear in the public rooms at lunchtime, partaking instead of light repasts in their bedchambers. The three young gentlemen, on the other hand, made their way to the dining room and ate heartily—Brandy less so than his two friends—then again settled themselves in the library to chat about the activities of their mutual acquaintances. It was not long before Rowan and the viscount were snoring lustily. Brandy sat musing for a time, listening to their contented rumblings. Then he rose thoughtfully to his feet and wandered out to the stables, where he procured a horse and rode off across the park. He had still not returned when the other guests assembled for dinner that evening in the white drawing room.

The weather had remained hot and sultry, and Lady Regina came downstairs feeling crosser than ever; but she brightened perceptibly at the sight of Viscount Landborough.

"Ah, Seffronia," she whispered to her sister, "if

there is one thing I find enchanting, it's a Vandyke beard. So distinguished, don't you agree?"

"He appears to be a most polished young man," Seffronia concurred.

As though to prove her words, Viscount Landborough came forward quickly and greeted them both with sumptuous bows.

"How delightful to meet you, sir," Regina caroled. "I believe your Aunt Honorée and I were girls together."

Landborough's brows contracted. "You know Aunt Honorée? Dreadful old biddy! But at last she's taken herself off to Gothgar Castle and hidden herself away, thank God, so we won't be subjected to her nonsense any longer. Can't tell you what a relief it is for the entire family to have her out of our hair!"

Regina drew back slightly and raised her eyebrows. "I had not realized . . ." she began, but Landborough cut in again.

"Perhaps you also knew the late demented chatelaine of Banbridge Hall, Lady Oriana Hemphill? She's gone off to live with Aunt Honorée, and that's another step forward for civilization, I can assure you!"

"The *late?*" Regina asked. Her mouth had grown tight. "Pray, what can you mean, sir? If she is deceased, how can she . . . ?"

He chuckled. "Just a little family joke, ma'am. Lady Oriana Hemphill . . ."

But before he could explain the intricacies of this witticism, Callie slipped into the room and moved quickly to her Aunt Seffronia's side. There was a moment of profound silence, then Landborough exhaled loudly.

"Well, indeed!" he exclaimed. "Who has been keeping this vision under wraps? She is precisely the sort of girl my mother has been prescribing for me; and while I've been searching ineffectually all over England—suffering untold agonies, I might add—someone has had her hidden away under his wing. Dillworth, no doubt, saving her for himself. I cry foul, Dillworth! Foul, I say!"

"Yes, well, er . . ." Rowan muttered. "Miss Belcroft, may I present an old chum of Brandy's and mine, Chipper Landborough? Er, that is . . . George Albert, I believe it is, Viscount Landborough."

The gentleman bent low over her hand, holding it lingeringly to his lips. "Your obedient servant, Miss Belcroft. Good God, such orbs! Will you do me the honor of becoming my bride?"

"Dash it all, Chipper!" Rowan protested. "You can't carry on like this under my roof."

"Not carrying on," Landborough assured him. "Mean every word of it."

Callie was staring unhappily down at her fan. "Please, sir," she protested, "this is a most inappropriate time . . ."

Regina let out a tinkle of laughter. "Come, come, child, put away these missish airs and enjoy yourself. Banter with Viscount Landborough—that is what he wishes. Say, 'Dear me, sir, your impetuosity is quite frightening, though thoroughly welcome'—something of that sort. Is that not the type of riposte you were hoping to receive, Lord Landborough?"

"Yes, yes," he agreed. "Most delightful! Though I shall then wish her to put her hand in mine, in a sweet, trusting way, and accept my offer."

"See here," Rowan growled, "you're not to propose marriage to Miss Belcroft. I've already asked her to be my wife."

"Has she accepted you?"

"Well, no . . . not yet."

"Then I shall press my suit and endeavor to steal her affections away from you."

"Dash it all, man! Do you mean to tell me that after accepting my hospitality—while still under my very roof—you are going to spend your time trying to lure my intended wife away from me?"

"Yes, I do," Landborough told him. "You know well enough that I have no conscience. No principles, either. I've decided to spend a few days with you, Dillworth." He beamed at Callie. "And if you could see your way clear to accepting me before Thursday, Miss Belcroft, I shall be able to drive you to Landborough Place and get my mother's blessing before she leaves to visit my sister in Bath. She'll be delighted with you, I assure you—you're just the sort of girl she's been wanting me to get leg-shackled with for some time."

Regina was watching her daughter curiously. "Is it true, Callie, that dear Rowan has made you an offer and you have not as yet given him an answer? That is heartless, indeed!"

"If we could settle everything and have the ceremony before the hunting season begins in earnest," Landborough continued, "we might have our honeymoon at Cavenleigh's box, and I would not be obliged to miss any of the delightful hunting they have in that country."

Callie fluttered her hands and tried to move away from him; but Landborough followed close beside her, bending his face near hers and making small clucking sounds. "My dear . . ." he began. Before he could go any further, Callie bowed her head and hurried out of the room.

Rowan scowled after her. "Now see what you've done, you bufflehead!"

"Indeed, I am sorry," Landborough admitted.

"Nonsensical girl," Regina muttered. "I've a notion to go after her and give her the scold of her life."

"No, no, dear lady," Landborough protested. "I stand at fault. I fear I've been a trifle heavy-handed. Such a delicate little creature—like a frail blossom. What she needs is something pretty to cheer her. Some flowers, perhaps. Do you have any fresh roses in your garden, old man? If your housekeeper could put together a nice bouquet for me, I'll coax Miss Belcroft out of her mopes in no time."

"No!" Rowan said firmly. "Dashed if I'm going to let you use my flowers to win my intended's heart away from me."

"Very well," Landborough said, undeterred. "Then I must think of another way. And this time I really must bring off a marriage; I've bungled three courtships already, and my mother does not even attempt to be civil to me anymore." He pulled thoughtfully at his mustache. "I realize that you have undoubtedly used all sorts of unfair tactics to

227

influence Miss Belcroft in your favor. No doubt lured her with your wealth . . ."

"Dash it all!" Rowan cried. "I have done no such thing!"

"Well, if it's wealth she likes," Landborough continued, ignoring his protests, "I am at a disadvantage, for although I've a tidy bit each year, I suspect that you've a good deal more, with the baskets of gold you've inherited from your uncle."

"Nonsense!" Rowan exclaimed. "I'll wager you're every bit as rich as I am."

"Really?" Landborough said. "I'll lay a monkey that I'm not."

"Very well," Rowan agreed. "A monkey it is. Though I'll be obliged to speak with my man of business before I can state the precise extent of my holdings."

"And I must also speak with my man on that head," Landborough told him.

Lady Regina, who had long since wearied of the conversation, began to fan herself vigorously with a bit of ivory and lace.

"Rowan, dear," she grumbled, "this house—it's remarkable what you're accomplishing with it, of course—but you must contrive somehow to improve the ventilation. Not a breath of air is passing through this room. I swear, one would think we were holding forth in a swamp."

"A swamp!" Rowan cried, his face rumpled with anxiety. "Surely, dear lady, it is not so bad as that! I shall call Foster to fetch a page with a palm frond.

Once you've been fanned properly, you'll feel as cool as Cleopatra."

"I wonder if I should make a quick dash home tonight," Landborough mused aloud. "I might fetch the sapphire ring with the baroque pearls that's such a famous and remarkable old family piece." He turned to Seffronia. "Do you think your niece would be lured by a bit of frippery such as that, Miss Valois?"

"No," Seffronia admitted. "I fear that her interests are far removed from material things."

Regina snorted. "I am confident you are mistaken, my dear sister. Any girl would be delighted to receive such a famous jewel as the Landborough sapphire."

"Any girl but Callie," Seffronia observed with a smile.

Regina was silent for a moment, then she sighed. "Perhaps you are right. She has no sense at all, the foolish child."

"Then I must devise a brilliant method for riveting her attention," Landborough went on. "If I were to write her a marvelous poem in the mode of a Shakespearean love sonnet . . . Something about raven eyes —that sort of thing. No, that won't fadge, I'm afraid, as her eyes are blue, are they not? Dash it all, don't believe I noted the color of her eyes."

"They are blue," Seffronia told him.

"Then it must be 'eyes as blue as azure pools.' "

"I don't think one should put *as* and *azure* together," Rowan pointed out. "Doesn't come out right with all those hissing sounds."

"Excellent suggestion," Landborough agreed. "I'll give the line more thought."

He called for a sheet of paper, a pen, and ink, which he carried to the dinner table with him and scratched upon from time to time, consulting his companions on each word he set down. By the time dinner was served, he had still not progressed past the first line, having been required to discard several promising flurries as being too similar to certain of Shakespeare's originals—the only differences being in the choice of articles and the placement of the punctuation.

When the party finally separated for the night, Brandy had still not returned, and Callie remained sequestered in her room, unresponsive to knocks on the door. Regina would have marched in and given her daughter a rousing lecture, but Seffronia prevailed upon her to let the matter—and the girl—rest until morning.

Rowan bid his guests good night, retreated to the library, and sinking wearily onto a chair, mopped his brow; and cursing friendship and courtship and all the other institutions which had landed him in his present predicament, he poured himself a generous glassful of brandy and set his mind to working his way out of his tangle.

He had slowly drained the glass and part of another, but was no closer to a solution, when he heard sounds in his vestibule.

"It's Brandy!" he exclaimed, leaping up in relief. "He will certainly know what to do." He scurried off down the hall to greet his friend.

To his surprise he found the vestibule overflowing with humanity. At first sight he thought there were several persons sweeping off their coats; but then he realized that it was only two: Brandy and—of all persons—Tristam, filling most of the room, smiling and happy.

"Tris!" Rowan cried with genuine pleasure. "How delighted I am to see you! How is your arm?"

"Coming along nicely, I am told," his friend said. "Though it is still quite useless in many ways."

Rowan put out a hand and pumped his friend's vigorously. "Well, I'm dashed happy to see you, old man. How fortunate that Brandy should encounter you on the road."

Belcroft smiled. "I did not meet him by accident, I must confess. I employed a considerable amount of cunning in finding him. I rode to Marcourt, lurked about the stables and gardens for a time, and finally sent a groom to deliver a confidential message. Fortunately the good man was trustworthy and delivered my words to none other than Tristam himself. The result is that you see him here before you. We have agreed not to conjecture on the reasons for our letters having gone astray."

"Yes, yes," Rowan agreed, "an excellent day's work! Come into the library and have something to refresh you."

They were striding across the central hall, laughing and bantering together, enjoying the best sort of camaraderie, when they all became aware of strange noises in the upper regions of the house—scampering sounds and squeaks of distress accompanied by loud exclamations. Brandy froze in his tracks at the bottom of the main staircase.

"Good God!" he muttered, and began leaping up the steps two at a time. Rowan and Tristam hurried after him, their faces anxious.

In the branching hallway that led into the west wing, Brandy discovered several doors open, one with his mother's head sticking out and another with Seffronia's. The door at the end of the hall was also open, and through it shone the light from a single candle. Without hesitation he sprinted toward it.

"Oh, thank God you're back!" Regina hissed as he sped past. "She is wandering again, and I could not march brazenly into young Landborough's room to rescue her."

As Brandy bounded into the bedchamber at the end of the hall, he found his sister standing in the middle of the floor, staring around herself in confusion. Landborough, a candy-striped nightcap flopping over one eye, was sitting up in his bed, holding a candle aloft.

"But, Miss Belcroft . . ." he was purring. "I should say Callie . . . angel . . ."

"Here, here, popsy," Brandy said gently, taking her by the arm and turning her around. "This way, my dear. Back to bed with you."

"Now wait," Landborough protested. "I realize this is some kind of mistake; but since she's come to me of her own free will, I should have an opportunity to further my suit if I can. Miss Belcroft, I've written you the most smashing poem! It goes: 'Shall I compare thee to a . . . a *spring* day?/ If I could write the beauty of your eyes,/ as blue as azure pools!' Lovely thought, don't you agree, despite the hissing?"

Setting his jaw, Brandy shoved his sister toward the door. Tristam and Rowan, both standing white-faced in the opening, silently stepped aside to let them pass.

Chapter 18

It was barely eight o'clock the following morning when the four young gentlemen met in the breakfast room. All were paler than usual and appeared to be in need of sleep. Landborough rubbed a hand wearily over his brow as he sank into a chair and sighed.

"I don't hesitate to tell you that I was devilish disappointed by your actions last night, Belcroft," he began. "I don't see how I'm going to overcome the advantages these other chaps have over me if no one will give me a chance. And just when I've found the girl who would precisely please my mother. And myself, of course . . ."

"No, no, Chipper," Rowan protested. "Couldn't have left her in your bedroom. Not the sort of thing at all. I must insist that Miss Belcroft be treated in a proper manner while she is under my roof."

Brandy was nodding thoughtfully to himself. "I can see that we shall be obliged to bring things out into the open; and by God, I say it should have been done long ago. As soon as the ladies join us, we'll make a clean breast of things once and for all."

Foster, who had entered during this speech, leaned over his master's shoulder.

"With your permission, sir, may I call your attention to this letter which Lady Belcroft left for you on her departure?" He held out a salver on which rested a folded sheet of paper.

"Departure?" Brandy asked in surprise. "Do you mean to tell me that my mother has actually risen at this ungodly hour and left Meadowmere?"

"Yes, sir. She entered her traveling carriage at approximately six o'clock and departed in the direction of Ollingsdown, so Mudget informed me."

"Where in heaven's name could she have been going?" Brandy wondered.

Rowan waved her letter in the air. "To a certain connection of Lady Bollinbridge's daughter, she says. Most gracious letter. Thanks me for my kindness and all that, and expresses regret at having been called away so suddenly." He laid the paper on the table.

Brandy sniffed. "Well, perhaps it's just as well. Her presence always makes my sister uneasy, despite my mother's efforts to be a soothing influence."

Foster cleared his throat. "Excuse me, sir, but Miss Belcroft also departed this morning."

Brandy and Tristam both rose to their feet.

"Departed!" Brandy exclaimed. "What are you saying?"

"She mounted Mr. Dillworth's young Arab mare and rode off toward the north."

"Now, just a moment," Brandy protested. "She rode to the north, and my mother rode to the south?"

"That is correct, sir."

"But it must have been their intention to join each other."

"Perhaps, sir. But Lady Belcroft departed at six A. M., while Miss Belcroft left only half an hour ago. I must add, sir, that Miss Belcroft appeared to be in a turbulent state of mind."

"Good God!" Rowan exclaimed, leaping to his feet. "Do you mean to tell me that no one attempted to stop her?"

"Sir," Foster said, assuming an icy facade, "no one with the authority to restrain her was present at the time of her departure. But Mudget has taken the liberty of saddling four of the fastest hunters in the event that anyone should wish to pursue her."

"By George, yes!" Rowan exclaimed. "We shall go after her, Brandy, shall we not?"

"Indeed yes!" Brandy agreed. "I have not the faintest notion what might be in her mind."

"Well," Landborough observed, yawning cavernously, "I may await you here instead of racing off across the countryside at this frightful hour."

"Certainly, Chipper," Rowan urged him. "You stay here. And remember that if there is anything you require to make yourself more comfortable, you need only ask. Consider the house your own."

At the stables Brandy quickly took command. "Tristam," he told his friend, "because of your tender arm, we shall give you the shortest route to follow. Ride to Tebblesdyke via Aldyce and meet me at the Bull. I shall take the longer way through Repping. And Rowan, I shall impose upon you to take the road south until you meet my mother, in the possibility that Callie might have ultimately gone to join her."

"But dash it all," their host protested. "She and I . . ."

"Please," Brandy urged. "Time is of the essence."

"Oh, very well," Rowan muttered. And quickly swinging a leg over one of the hunters, he cantered out of the stableyard.

With some difficulty Tristam hoisted himself onto the back of the largest hunter. Brandy, springing onto a third, rode out to the main road alongside his friend, where they parted, each cantering off rapidly along his prescribed course.

An hour later they met at the Bull in Tebblesdyke.

"She passed along the route I followed," Tristam told his friend. "I spoke to several persons who saw her."

"Aye, indeed," one of the ostlers agreed as he took their horses, "she rode past here half an hour ago or more. A beautiful lady in a blue riding dress. But she looked most unhappy, sir."

"Half an hour," Brandy mused. "We should be able to overtake her quickly if she is on that little mare of Rowan's."

They paused to refresh themselves, each downing a hot mug of tea and a slice of cold beef between two chunks of bread. Then they remounted and proceeded on their quest together.

"Is it possible that she is on her way home?" Tristam asked his companion after they had followed Callie's trail for another hour and a half. "This is the route I took when I traveled from Marcourt to Colter Abbey in August."

Brandy sighed. "It would seem so, indeed. If I could be sure . . . But I feel that I must catch up with her and be reassured as to her mental state."

"Of course," Tristam agreed. They urged their horses forward at a faster pace.

It soon became apparent to them, however, that they were not gaining on their quarry. Each village they passed produced at least one witness who had seen the "most beautiful lady" ride by; but always Brandy and Tristam were informed that she had been by "at least half an hour ago, sir. No, that little white mare of hers did not appear winded. No, sir; no lather on her neck."

When they finally arrived at Colter Abbey, dusk had fallen; the house was ablaze with lights. Rimpson threw the front door open and, wreathed in smiles, exclaimed, "Ah, Master Brandon! Welcome home, sir! And Lord Tristam!" He bowed majestically.

"What's this?" Brandy asked him. "Is my sister here?"

"Yes, sir. Retired to her room. And her ladyship has returned—much to his lordship's delight, I am happy to inform you. Lord Osgood has not been quite himself during his separation from her ladyship."

"The devil you say!" Brandy exclaimed. "Did my sister and mother arrive together?"

"No, sir. Her ladyship arrived two hours ago, and

Miss Callie only just rode into the yard and went straight to her room."

With Tristam close behind him, Brandy strode rapidly across the great hall and into a small side parlor which was sending shafts of candlelight and squeaks of rasping music through its open door. To his surprise he found old Bascomb, a groom who had been an excellent fiddler in his day, perched on a stool in a corner, scraping a lively country dance on his ancient violin while Lord and Lady Belcroft, their arms entwined around each other's waists, were treading the measures up and down the room, pausing occasionally to clutch each other in a desperate manner and exchange urgent kisses.

"My dearest one," Regina murmured, "you are the most enchanting dancer in the entire world."

"And you," he assured her, "are the most delightful, most exquisite . . ."

He pulled her hard against his breast and pressed trembling lips to her mouth. Then he began to cover her face and throat with passionate kisses.

"Sir!" Brandy protested. "Mama!"

His parents leaped apart, both scowling at him guiltily.

"What the devil are you doing here?" Osgood snapped.

"I'm looking for my sister, sir."

Regina giggled. "She is at Meadowmere, you goose."

"No, Mama, we have followed her here. Rimpson saw her arrive."

"Then deal with Rimpson," Regina told him airily

and turned back with a smile toward her husband. "We shall allow these children to solve their own problems, shall we not, my love?"

"Yes, yes," Osgood agreed. "Our efforts have accomplished very little in the past. Let us see how well they can manage for themselves."

With a preoccupied nod in the direction of their son and his friend they turned away and, beaming at each other, walked out through a far door, hand in hand.

Brandy sighed. "It is just as well that they will not be with us when we speak to Callie. My parents have a disquieting effect on my sister."

"But let's find her quickly," Tristam urged. "Why did she run away? Is there any chance she may do herself harm?"

"I have no way of knowing," Brandy admitted.

The two young men strode out into the central hallway and sprang quickly up the staircase. After several rapid steps along a branching corridor they reached the girl's door.

"Callie," Brandy called, tapping lightly on the upper panel, "are you there?"

They waited for a moment, listening, but there was no response. Brandy knocked louder.

"Callie!"

When there was still no answer, he turned an alarmed face toward Tristam. "Perhaps we should force the door."

At that moment a grizzled old woman in an apron and white cap came hobbling around a corner.

"Ah, it's you, love," she called. "I've sent for Big

William to force the door. Miss Callie won't answer me."

"How long has she been in there, Nurse?"

"Not long, but time enough to lose more blood than she can spare."

"Good God!" Tristam exclaimed, turning to place his sound shoulder against the door. "Hold the knob open, Brandy. I'll break it down."

He drew back, then hurled his weight against the door, and it burst open with a rending pop, rebounding against the inside wall. Callie, barely visible in the light from the hallway, was slumped at her dressing table, her face buried in her arms. In two steps Brandy was at her side, pulling her roughly to her feet.

"Callie!" he gasped. "Have you done yourself mischief? Taken poison or anything rash?"

"No, no," she said, trying to pull away from him. "Only leave me. I have withdrawn from the world. I shall never venture out of this room again—even if I should live to be one hundred years old."

Marching in through the open door, Nurse began to light the wall sconces.

"No, please don't!" Callie protested. "No light!" She waved a hand in front of her brother's face. "And please take Lord Tristam away. I cannot bear to think of the disgust he must feel for me at this moment."

She slipped out of Brandy's grasp and sank back onto her chair, burying her face again in her arms. The two young men stood considering the back of her head, each wrestling with his own thoughts as old Nurse bustled over to her charge.

"Well, now," she commanded, "you two can just run along and let me deal with miss. I'll have her tucked into her bed, snug and warm, before she has time to take a chill."

Tristam slowly turned his head to observe the heavy wooden grills across the windows and the other prisonlike features of the room. On the dressing table, beyond the tips of Callie's limp fingers, the figure of Lady Godiva was propped against an ancient lead crystal mirror. Tristam took the puppet in his hand.

"Such a day that was," he said half to himself as memories of Bartholomew Fair flooded through his mind. "Wonderful halcyon day of hope . . ."

His vision began to blur. Unable to resist the rush of emotion that welled up inside him, he laid a hand gently on Callie's shining hair.

"The madness is growing worse, is it not?"

Brandy looked at him curiously. "No," he said, "I had thought she was much better of late. And I would certainly not call it *madness*. I blame my parents for Callie's affliction—she did not begin sleepwalking until recently, when their quarrels grew so violent, and she only walks now when she is profoundly disturbed."

Tristam stared at him, his mouth sliding open. *"Sleepwalking!"*

"Yes," Brandy continued. "Such a worrisome affliction. We never know when she might wander out a window or fall down a staircase and be seriously injured."

"But is that the full extent of her malady?"

"Of course. What else?"

"Then why did your Aunt Seffronia imply that she was mad?"

"Good God!" Brandy exclaimed, profoundly shocked. "I cannot believe she did so."

Tristam stood looking from one to the other. "Sleepwalking!" He tried to laugh but only managed a rasping sound. "That's all that's wrong!" He wagged his head. "You see! I told them that her mind was as sound as yours or mine."

"Of course," Brandy agreed, "but . . ."

Tristam rubbed a hand distractedly across his face. "When I think of the suffering . . . the indecision . . ."

"I don't understand," Brandy said; but Tristam was not listening to him. Dropping to his knees beside Callie's dressing table, he pulled her roughly into his arms.

"Callie," he began, "what are your feelings for me?" Then he shook his head impatiently. "No, no, that's not the way to start; I must tell you first of my feelings for you. I love you—have loved you since that night we walked together in the garden."

Callie slid her arms around his neck.

"Do you feel any affection at all for me?" he continued. "Do you think you could ever find it in your heart to consider my suit?"

"You great thick-headed looby!" Brandy exploded. "Stop talking and kiss the girl! Can't you see that everything is settled?"

Catching hold of the nurse's hand, he dragged her toward the door. "We must leave them alone now," he told her. "I still do not fully understand this affair, but from this point on, if they cannot work things out for themselves, there is no hope for them."

The following morning, glowing with happiness, Callie and Tristam met in the great hall and made their way toward the little solarium for breakfast. As they passed a small dark anteroom, the gray cat sidled out and wound itself, purring, between Tristam's feet.

"I shall treat you more kindly today," the marquis promised him. He leaned down and passed a hand over the animal's silky head.

"Yes, dear old Biscuit," Callie murmured. "I shall miss him when I am gone."

Leading her lover down a short, unprepossessing hallway, then around a corner and up a narrow flight of steps, she guided him into the bright little breakfast room. Osgood was seated at one end of the table, humming cheerfully to himself as he sipped at a coffee cup and helped himself to generous portions of buttered eggs.

"Ah, good morning," he called, beaming at them. Then, as he saw the extent of Callie's blushes, he crowed with pleasure. "Well, my angel, you are in excellent looks since your visit to Meadowmere. I shall send you there immediately if you ever again begin to grow peaked."

"No, Papa," she protested with a shy laugh, "you do not understand. It is not Meadowmere which has caused me such happiness."

"What then?" he demanded.

"Sir," Tristam began, clearing his throat, "it is my most heartfelt wish that you will give me permission to approach your daughter and ask her to be my wife."

"By George!" Osgood exclaimed. "If she is willing, I assure you that nothing could give me more pleasure."

Regina put her head in through the doorway. "Ah," she chirped, "so you have worked things out between you. I could not be more delighted!"

Stepping briskly into the room, she beamed at Tristam, gave her husband an impudent wink, and proceeded airily toward her place at the table. But as she passed Osgood's chair, her toe caught in a fold of rumpled carpet, and with a cry of dismay she pitched forward, landing on an elbow in her husband's buttered eggs, her free hand scattering salt cellars and condiments in all directions. Osgood's cup of coffee bounded into his lap. The unfortunate man let out a scream of pain and leaped to his feet, clutching at his thigh.

"My leg!" he cried. "You clumsy hag, you've spilled scalding coffee on my leg!"

Regina gasped. "Clumsy hag!"

"You crone!" he shouted.

Her chin jutted. Grasping a nearby cream pitcher, she dumped the contents over his head.

"Good God!" Brandy protested, appearing at that

245

moment in a doorway and rushing forward to restrain his parents.

"You bully!" Regina shrieked.

"Papa!" Brandy pleaded. "Mama! Will this never end?"

"Never!" Regina cried. "Unless this loathsome man will abandon his savage ways."

"Savage? Ha, ha!" Osgood roared. "I am infinitely more civilized than yourself, madam!"

"Please," Brandy urged. "Come away, Mama. I'll take you back to town. You must not continue this unproductive relationship when you will be able to enjoy such a happy, entertaining life as soon as the Season begins."

"What! Be driven from my home by this Machiavelli! Never!"

"Your home!" Osgood shouted. "It is *my* home!"

"It is also *my* home, sir. And if you attempt to drive me from it, I shall be happy to meet you in a court of law. In fact, I should like nothing better!" Regina tossed her head.

Osgood picked up a napkin and made a cursory swipe at the cream which was oozing from his locks. "I shall deal with you presently, virago!" Wagging a finger at his wife, he hurried off in search of his valet. Regina gave a snort of satisfaction and marched to her place, settling herself majestically and sweeping back a stray tress with a graceful hand.

"That odious creature!" she muttered. "He is raising all these horrid rows with no object in mind but to ruin my complexion." She turned to Brandy. "Is my face hideously flushed, my love?"

"Flushed?" Brandy stammered. "Good God, Mama, how can you think of your appearance at a time like this?"

"Because it is my beauty which your father appreciates most. And my spirit, of course."

"Your spirit?" Brandy closed his mouth and stared at his mother. "Do you mean to tell me that all this rioting is mere sham?"

"No, no, certainly not! How can you ask such a question after witnessing your father's unforgivable behavior? But I shall bring him into line, you may be sure of that. Within the hour I shall have him eating out of my hand."

She turned to her white-faced daughter. "Well, Callie, my love, I know how you dislike all this; but you shall see how it is when you and Tristam are married. You'll find yourself hurling teacups and cursing each other when you've lived together a few years."

With a squeak of despair Callie clapped a hand over her mouth and ran out of the room. Tristam raced after her. His long legs carried him quickly to her side, and catching her around the waist, he swung her through a doorway into a small sitting room and pulled her down onto a sofa beside him.

"Callie," he protested, "you know your mother speaks only for herself and your father. I could never bring myself to curse you, and I am confident you will never hurl a teacup at me."

"No, certainly not, but . . ." She hesitated long enough to wipe a tear away with the back of a hand. "How can we be sure?"

"We must trust ourselves," he said. "My mother and father never exchanged an uncivil word within my hearing. I am confident we have it in our power to be as kind and affectionate as they were. Your mother and father—well . . ."

Callie shook her head miserably. "I could not bear it if we turned out to be such inveterate gladiators."

"Nor I," he agreed. "But you are not like your mother, and I am not like your father. In fact, I am not even like my own father."

They sat quietly for a moment, both thinking deeply. Finally Callie relaxed against him.

"Besides," he continued, "how could I ever be less than euphoric when He has bestowed such perfection?"

Epilogue

Everyone who knew the Waiverings agreed that their marriage was probably one of the happiest in England. The young couple spent every hour of the day and night in each other's company, and the servants were constantly on tenterhooks to avoid catching them locked in ardent embrace behind a drawing-room curtain or in the shrubbery of the more secluded sections of the garden. Brandy, who made frequent visits to Marcourt, was delighted by the happy tenor of their life; and it was with the greatest satisfaction that he received the assurance that his sister no longer walked in her sleep.

In the spring of 1820, however, conditions outside the home began to infringe upon their wedded bliss. Unrest continued among the working classes throughout the nation, and although Tristam had constructed some excellent residential blocks to house his mill families and had made every effort to insure wholesome working conditions, he eventually found it necessary to visit his factories and meet with his employees to work out certain grievances and misunderstandings.

He was naturally reluctant to be parted from his

bride for even so much as a minute, and it occurred to him that she might be willing to accompany him. But he reminded himself that the weather was still exceedingly cold and that Callie's fragile constitution might suffer from such a taxing journey. After arguing with himself for several hours he decided to let her decide for herself whether she wished to endure such hardships in order to be with him.

"I am obliged to travel into Yorkshire," he told her. "I dread the thought of being separated from you for three whole days, and I would invite you to accompany me, but the trip is arduous, and I fear it may be harmful to your health."

Callie stared down at the tips of her toes, blinked away her tears, then turned a brave, smiling face to him.

"Of course, I shall miss you very much while you are gone," she told him. "Please give me your promise that you will exert every effort to keep yourself safe and well."

He nodded, took one of her hands to squeeze between his own two, and quickly turned away to hide his disappointment. Shortly thereafter he climbed into his brougham and set off on his journey.

That night the weather turned unseasonably warm, and as there was no moon, a band of free traders chose the time to move a shipment of goods from one station to the next. There was a point on their route where the woods were bisected by the highroad, and the smugglers hid among the brambles to reconnoiter before making their dash across to the shelter on the other side.

A gentle breeze was blowing, rustling the leaves around their feet and the hair on the backs of their necks. They listened, holding their breath, and immediately became aware of the steady *clop, clop, clop* of an approaching horse. Suddenly, from behind the curtain of foliage, rode a lady, her body white and luminous in the darkness and her long flowing blond hair draped demurely over her. The brigands gasped.

"Great God in heaven, preserve us!" one of them hissed. "We're set upon by spirits, by way o' punishment."

The leader nodded. "Aye, 'tis Lady Godiva 'erself, nekked as a turnip, an' her dead these nine hun'red year. A punishment, for sure."

But to their surprise the ghost passed by them and disappeared around the next bend in the road. The leader scratched his head.

" 'Twas, perhaps, a sign, lads. But what kind? That's the puzzle. Can ye tell me why this specter we seen—this Lady Godiva—be the spit an' image o' the young Marchioness o' Waivering?"

THE DARK HORSEMAN

Marianne Harvey

author of *The Proud Hunter*

Beautiful Donna Penroze had sworn to her dying father that she would save her sole legacy, the crumbling tin mines and the ancient, desolate estate *Trencobban*. But the mines were failing, and Donna had no one to turn to. No one except the mysterious Nicholas Trevarvas—rich, arrogant, commanding. Donna would do anything but surrender her pride, anything but admit her irresistible longing for *The Dark Horseman*.

A Dell Book $3.25

THE WILD ONE

by
MARIANNE HARVEY

bestselling author of *The Dark Horseman*
and *The Proud Hunter*

Proud, beautiful Judith—raised by her stern
grandmother on the savage Cornish coast—
boldly abandoned herself to one man and sought
solace in the arms of another. But only one man
could tame her, could match her fiery spirit,
could fulfill the passionate promise of rapturous,
timeless love.

A Dell Book $2.95   (19207-2)

The passionate sequel to
the scorching novel of
fierce pride and forbidden love

THE PROUD HUNTER

by Marianne Harvey

Author of *The Dark Horseman*
and *The Wild One*

Trefyn Connor—he demanded all that was his—and
more—with the arrogance of a man who fought to
win ... with the passion of a man who meant to pos-
sess his enemy's daughter and make her pay the
price!

Juliet Trevarvas—the beautiful daughter of The Dark
Horseman. She would make Trefyn come to her. She
would taunt him, shock him, claim him body and soul
before she would surrender to THE PROUD HUNTER.

A Dell Book $3.25   (17098-2)

Love—the way you want it!

Candlelight Romances

Dell Bestsellers